ANTimatter

David Winship

Copyright © 2018 David Winship

All rights reserved.

"We step out of our solar system into the universe seeking only peace and friendship, to teach if we are called upon, to be taught if we are fortunate."

Kurt Waldheim (The Voyager Golden Record)

"There are those who look at things the way they are, and ask why. I dream of things that never were, and ask why not?"

Bobby Kennedy

Contents

THE RECEPTION COMMITTEE 8

NO PLACE LIKE HOME 28

WHERE ARE THE TOILETS? 43

ENCOUNTER WITH A BLANID 48

POINT OF NO RETURN 55

THE PUNCTURED BALL 62

PIGEON OF PEACE 84

THE LIMITS OF THE DIPLOMATIC ARENA 97

LIFTED 117

COMPOS MENTIS 135

ANOTHER BAR, ANOTHER BRAWL 152

THE QUANDARY 162

PIGEON OF DISCONTENT 173

MARCH OF THE PENGUINS 186

DISCLOSURE 211

SOME DAYS YOU'RE THE PIGEON… 221

WE ARE FAMILY 234

THE RECEPTION COMMITTEE

"Oh my god. This is gonna be weird. It's like we're inside a glow-worm!"

"You don't get glow-worms in outer space."

"It's twisting and… uh, wait, it's getting smaller. And darker. Maybe we're inside some kind of ghastly space bobbit worm."

"What the 'ell's a bobbit worm?"

"I used to have one in my fish tank. Uh oh. It's got *very* dark. Woh-oh-oh-oh-aaaaaarghhh! Now we're on the *outside* of it!"

"It's not a bobbit worm."

"Are we dead or alive right now? Is this like Schrödinger's box? What do people think? Am I dead or alive?"

"Both, if you ask me. And it's obviously not a box."

"I mean, y'know, conceptually? Wait, I can see a light! There's a pinpoint of light straight up ahead."

"Don't say it. Please don't say there's a light at the end of the tunnel."

"Uh oh! Oh no!"

"What is it?"

"Damn!"

If you're going to travel by wormhole, don't be drinking beer and eating crisps. I found that out the hard way. So, yeah, wormhole travel - popping down one of those ol' cosmological plugholes. What did I imagine it to be like? To be honest, when we set out from Earth, heading for the small circumbinary planet known as Smolin9 in the Andromeda galaxy, I was clueless. I had absolutely no idea what to expect. Well, of course, I'd made an assumption or two. Everyone does, don't they? So, this was *my* main assumption: I thought it'd be like sailing through a trippy, swirling, psychedelic tunnel while floaty orchestral melodies competed with choral chanting in a soul-caressing abstract audio soup. With maybe a bit of the outro to the Beatles' 'Day In The Life' thrown in for good measure. I fully realise that that depiction may not be as good as some of the ones you encounter in the movies and stuff, but hey. Anyway, whatever. As it turns out, wormhole travel isn't anything like that at all. There's a tunnel, yes. But sometimes you're inside it and sometimes you're kind of riding on the outside of it. Nothing is even remotely psychedelic and there is definitely no music. Nothing could have been further removed from my expectation.

The closest analogy I can come up with is that it's like being propelled into the steepest bend and drop on a roller coaster. And you're not strapped in. And there's no hand rail. Okay, I'll admit it, I've never actually *been* on a roller coaster. But I've been on a simulator. Anyway, regardless whether real or simulated, traveling by wormhole is actually like going on a roller coaster that just plain refuses to flatten out. Well, I suppose worse things happen in space – with wormholes, at least it's not rocket science, so you don't burn up on re-entry.

Wait, I mustn't get ahead of myself. I mentioned the Andromeda Galaxy, right? Well, actually, the Andromeda Galaxy is really the M31. No, seriously, if we're going to be precise (and we are), the Andromeda Galaxy is known to astronomers as Messier 31 or M31. I know this because I worked on a project known as RECONNECT. It was established in 2090 to seek out signals from intelligent extra-terrestrial civilisations. My role had provided me with quite a bit of detailed knowledge about M31, a vast cosmic dance that I might otherwise have confused with a Bracknell bypass. But I tell you what, I couldn't say any of that knowledge had proved particularly useful up to that point. But just to show that I'd paid *some* attention to what my scientist colleagues had told me, I'll tell you some stuff about it. M31 is big. I mean literally big. It boasts around a trillion stars, compared with the Milky Way which only has around two to four hundred billion. With an apparent magnitude of 3.4, it's bright enough to be seen from Earth with the naked eye on moonless nights. Without wishing to alarm you, I should point out that M31 is approaching the Milky Way at a rate of around 68 miles per second and, in a mere three or four billion years' time, the two will merge to form a single giant elliptical galaxy. So, don't say I didn't warn you! To help you prepare for this momentous event, I'll maybe provide some more background information later. Actually, now I think about it, the planet may be in a different constellation. Cygnus, possibly. Yes, sorry, it's Cygnus. So, it's okay, you can forget about Andromeda and all that doomsday stuff. Besides, we've got about three and a half billion years to come up with an escape plan before the two galaxies collide.

. . .

As I tried to haul myself to my feet, it was like my legs just melted underneath me. My landing gear was toast!

"Oh my god!" Aysha exclaimed. "That was 'orrendous!"

I nodded and yawned. For some reason, neither of

us could stop yawning. I also had a headache and my vision was blurry. "It was like... hmm, it was like..." At that point, the roller coaster analogy hadn't occurred to me and I couldn't express what it was like at all. It was about as definable as love or the human condition or those witty ripostes that disappear as soon as you need them.

"Well," Aysha interrupted, "I s'pose you'd expect some physical discomfort when you get sucked into a dimensional anomaly in the time-space continuum, wouldn't you? Anyway, it's all over now."

"Is it though? If it was time travel, perhaps it's in the future," I objected, flinching as she aimed a punch at my shoulder. The roller coaster analogy now careered into my head at a frightening speed. "Yeah, you feel like screaming, but you don't have a voice. In fact, it's kind of like you don't even have a *body*, let alone a voice. And then there's that moment when you realise it's definitely not just a simulator."

Aysha regarded me with a quizzical look. And yawned. "A simulator?" she queried. "What the 'ell are you talkin' about? By the way, you *were* screamin'. And shoutin' out. I could 'ear you all the time."

"Oh?"

"Yeah, she said, "At least, I assume that was you callin' out for a pillow and a blanket? And a vodka and orange? And, uh, barf bags?"

I nodded. That had been right at the start of the trip, before the whole thing had got seriously scary and weird, before everything had become stripped of tangible reality, before we'd been bombarded with sense stimuli - sounds, images, smells, tastes. None of it had offered any kind of coherent narrative, none of it had fitted into a rational pattern. Were those even *external* stimuli? I didn't know. I couldn't tell. Some other pretty bad stuff happened too. Unsavoury stuff. Don't make me go there. Before long, my brain had started to lose its grip. Memories had started flashing by in a Groundhog Day loop of random recollected moments. To give you an example of what I mean - my dog died eight times during the trip!

Years later, I described the experience to someone in a bar who flatly refused to believe it. He told me that what I had experienced was a common psychic phenomenon – the 'falling dream'. It is, he explained, an indication of insecurity, instability or anxiety. In some aspect of my waking life, he told me, I must have felt emotionally overwhelmed or unsafe or out of control. According to this guy, a falling dream may also reflect a sense of failure or inferiority, a feeling that you don't measure up to people's expectations. Not content with that, he launched into a spirited exposition of Freudian theory and accused me of the most arcane urges and impulses imaginable. He seemed particularly keen to establish how I had landed. Had I landed on my back? Or had my hands broken my fall? Or had I landed in water?

Well, the thing is, it *wasn't* a dream, falling or otherwise, and, when the spheroidal mouth of the wormhole had finally disgorged us, there we were - sprawled out on a heavily textured grey magma floor, yawning like basking seals. I noticed Aysha's face was swollen and puffy as if she'd just gone twelve rounds in a boxing ring. Her eyes were red as if she had been crying for hours, but there was no evidence of any tears.

"It was like being turned inside out!" I said, still struggling to exercise some control over my legs.

"Yeah, okay," said Aysha, grimacing slightly at my exaggeration.

I was all like roller coasters and barf bags and dead dogs and being turned inside out. How could Aysha behave like we had just stepped off a number 26 bus? "Like being turned inside out!" I repeated, determined to get more of a reaction. "And feeling incredibly itchy all over and you can't scratch it because..."

"'Cause your skin's on the inside?" Aysha suggested.

"Yeah. And your internal organs are on the *outside*!" I was starting to relish the hyperbole now. "And all the loose change comes out of your pockets! Yeah, that's the worst bit - all your loose change comes out and coins are like flying around, hitting your organs! And you're like, hey, I've lost all my change!"

Aysha looked at me askance. "Hmm. Really?" Hauling herself to her feet, she frowned at me. "Your loose change? Don't you think if you'd been turned inside out, you might 'ave more to worry about than losin' your loose change? Anyway, it's not *you* that gets turned inside out. It's space-time itself. In a wormhole, space-time is so curved that it kinda doubles back on itself."

I stood up, took a slow and overly exaggerated stride and said, "That's one small step for…" It was one giant dig in the ribs for me as Aysha put paid to my clowning around. I don't know if it was the blow from her fist or all the talk about barf bags, but a pang of nausea welled up and I started sweating profusely. The weightlessness you encounter during wormhole travel completely confuses your body. Your inner ear cannot reliably judge up from down and your balance gets thrown out of whack. I moved my head too quickly, my stomach flipped and before I could do anything about it, my whole body heaved and I was back on my knees, vomiting like crazy.

. . .

I suppose I should tell you a bit about how we came to be in this pickle. And it wasn't by means of any contraption I'd built in my garden shed. As I mentioned before, I'd been involved in a project on Earth called RECONNECT, conceived to facilitate scientific research into intelligent alien life in the wake of my grandmother's encounters with extra-terrestrials during the early part of the twenty-first century.

Actually, I need to take you back a bit further in time. Some of you may be aware that Voyager 1 was launched by NASA way back in 1977? Well, that space probe, along with its golden record containing greetings, pictures and audio-visual information from Earth, eventually got picked up by a pair of itinerant spacecombers from a planet known as Morys Minor. As a direct consequence, one of them, smolin9, visited Earth to determine its suitability for colonisation. Fortunately, or unfortunately, depending on your perspective, our beloved planet got rejected, because, apparently (and, I suppose, not surprisingly), it exceeded volatility thresholds. You're not going to believe this, but during his time on Earth, smolin9 married my grandmother, Melinda Hill of Camden in London, and the pair of them travelled by wormhole to Morys Minor. To her amazement, she was obliged to undergo a surgical procedure relating to her heart tissue (essential for the production of special blue blood cells required for survival on the planet). She didn't find out until it was too late, but such operations were irreversible. It meant she could not return to Earth, unless she could find a Mortian heart donor - apparently, Mortian hearts function perfectly on both Morys Minor *and* Earth. Luckily, the situation resolved itself when an extraordinary set of misunderstandings led to smolin9's associate, polkingbeal67, swapping hearts with her.

You're still with me, right? Well, her situation became even stranger when, for some curious reason, the ancient, ailing Mortian leader decided to name her (my grandmother) as his successor. Long story short, a random series of events led to the tragic death of smolin9, and the planet was subsequently renamed in his honour. Some time later, after thwarting an attempted subjugation of her adopted planet by chilloks - highly developed, diminutive creatures evolved from ants – my grandmother returned to Earth. And polkingbeal67 became the new leader of Smolin9. That all makes perfect sense, right? You're following me okay?

. . .

Yukawa3, who had accompanied us on the wormhole trip, was a native of this new temporary home planet of ours and a seasoned veteran of wormhole travel. He had assumed his native Mortian form, but it didn't alarm me – I'd seen him this way before. Mortians are small naked humanoids, no more than five feet tall, with disproportionately large heads, hands and feet. Oily, luminous, almost translucent skin covers their light, spindly frames and wide, lustrous oily-black eyes with greyish pupils dominate the exaggerated facial contours. They have no visible ears and sometimes their mouths keep opening and closing as if they're gasping for breath. Think H.G. Wells and the Morlocks and then multiply it by a comically gruesome factor of quite a lot. He handed us each a vial of water. Except that it *wasn't* water. It *clearly* wasn't water because it smelt like a burning tyre filled with rotten eggs.

Aysha pushed it away. "No thanks," she said. "What I need is some chicken soup."

"Drink it!" he insisted. "It's HDA. I hope that answers your question. You *have* to take it."

HDA. Oh, yes, now I remembered. We had ingested some of this foul-tasting liquid before we had set out from Earth. HDA stood for Homeodynamic Disruption Antidote and it tasted like, well, burning rubber and rotten eggs.

"You like it?" asked yukawa3.

"Er, yeah," I said, almost gagging. "In theory."

"By the way," he said, "you'll be pleased and honoured and humbled to know that the planet has had another change of name and it now goes by the name of your grandmother."

I don't think I could have been more astonished if he'd mutated into a hippopotamus and started dancing the flamenco. "This planet is called 'Mrs Hill'?"

"Melinda. It's called Melinda in honour of your grandmother."

I suppose I *should* have felt pleased and honoured and humbled, but I was too bewildered and confused and preoccupied with my wormhole travel sickness. "Why? Why have you changed it? Why my grandmother? Why does this planet keep changing its name?"

Looking around, I noticed we were standing in a large magma chamber, illuminated by clusters of reddish orbs. Nearby, a pale, slimy, elongated face peered studiously at a kind of control panel, misshapen fingers twitching feverishly over a bank of screens displaying rapidly scrolling hieroglyphics. Yukawa3 introduced the stranger as casimir2 but offered no further elucidation. Unfailingly polite, I offered my hand. The first thing I noticed was the firm handshake. The second thing I noticed was the thin odorous fluid secreting from rubbery protuberances on his fingers. As I made a mental note to try noticing things in a different order in future, Aysha and I just stared, entranced.

Aysha whispered to me. "Do you suppose they 'ave any idea how ugly their children are gonna be?"

The two Mortians hesitated for a moment and then conferred together in their native tongue. Like a runaway train gathering speed, the conversation soon became animated and yukawa3's expression distorted into confusion and then into horror.

"Everything okay?" I asked tentatively. The question landed like a glass of water on an oil fire. Their voices became even more agitated.

Unimpressed, Aysha stiffened, folded her arms in protest and coughed loudly to catch their attention. To no avail. Judging by the way yukawa3 was flapping his arms around, like a fledgling bird desperately attempting a maiden flight, it would appear that casimir2 was delivering some unwelcome news.

Aysha muttered something about the planet clearly lacking the capacity to sustain intelligent life as we knew it. I could see what she meant. Clearly, nothing was going to calm or distract yukawa3 or casimir2 for the time being.

If we had been expecting some sort of ceremony to mark our arrival, those expectations were disappearing like worms in a piranha tank. So, no twenty-one-gun salute, nobody in silk vestments, no formal introductions, no lavish buffet and no flash photography. No ticker tape or baskets of fruit from the local Mortian village. No local dignitaries and their families agog with excitement. Nothing. Surely it wouldn't have hurt to put up a few streamers? It didn't *feel* like we were the first man and woman to boldly go where no man or woman had ever been before.

I took Aysha's arm and we walked unsteadily towards an oval-shaped doorway in the magma surround. It struck me that the surface gravity was remarkably similar to that of Earth. "What do you think's going on?" I asked her.

"Search me," she said. "Hey, though... What about *that*? We've just been in a worm'ole! We're on another flamin' *planet*! Hey, I'm an astronaut! I can't believe it! And look at me, I'm wearin' jeans, for crissakes!"

"Yes, I know." I bit my lip in a mixture of pleasure and pain, anxiety and delight, a cloud of doubt scudding across my mind like one of those clouds that are thick underneath and fluffy on top like a wedding cake or something. "Just so long as we can get *back* again!" Suddenly, I was really missing even the worst aspects of life on Earth. Joni Mitchell was right - you don't know what you've got till it's gone. "Aysha, tell me, seriously, are you as terrified as I am?"

"Pull yourself togevver, Neil, dammit!" she admonished me.

She was right. I quickly pondered the ramifications of space travel and concluded that the physical aspect of it is only half the challenge. About eighty percent of it is mental. Let's face it, this was an opportunity to demonstrate man's indomitable spirit in the face of crushing adversity. And I didn't like the notion of getting crushed by adversity, or anything else, so I steeled myself indomitably for the challenges that lay ahead. "Don't worry, I'm up for this," I assured her. "After all, my grandmother was an intergalactic traveller. I've got space in my blood."

"You've also got it between yer ears!" said Aysha scornfully. "Jus' cos your face looks serious, don't mean yer bein' sensible. Hey, this place is a bit underwhelming, isn't it?"

I looked around. She was right. It needed a lick of paint. And a carpet. A few throw pillows wouldn't have gone amiss either.

"Were we supposed to bring our own chairs?" said Aysha. And then her voice tailed off. Eyebrows arched in surprise, she was peering intently at something over my shoulder. "O-k-a-y," she intoned slowly, as if she was trying out the word for the first time. "That's w-e-i-r-d."

"What's weird?" I asked, spinning around towards the rough-hewn opening in the wall. I smiled brightly - I've no idea why, but I suppose it could have been the HDA kicking in. Quite honestly, the sight that met my eyes did not warrant a smile at all. No more than ten yards away, two apparently human earthling forms were crouching in the shadows, pointing strange twin-barrelled alien firearms at us. So, yes, that *was* weird.

Well, here was my first serious brush with adversity. A courageous person would have reacted in a calm and appropriate manner. A courageous person would have managed to stifle the involuntary shriek that issued from the bottom of my soul before I clutched Aysha's sleeve in abject terror. Well, you know what? I don't care. Personally, I think courage is overrated. If we hadn't wasted so many centuries worshipping gods, sports, alcohol and courage, we could perhaps have developed some really *useful* stuff like invisibility cloaks and shape-shifting. And, at that moment, I'm sure Aysha was fully on board with those sentiments. Possibly. I don't know. What I knew was that the novelty of all this was starting to wear off.

The two armed men rushed straight past us like we weren't even there. One of them fired some kind of laser beam at the wall above yukawa3's head, causing the magma to sputter languidly for a few seconds before it subsided like a pricked balloon. As casimir2 raised his hands in a gesture of peevish surrender, yukawa3 dropped to the floor like a pancake missing the pan. After a few seconds, he opened one eye tentatively to peer at the source of the shooting and then promptly shut it tight again.

"Get up!" barked one of the men, a tall swarthy individual with a callous expression in his eyes. He aimed a kick at yukawa3's torso, which the latter evaded by adroitly flexing his back. A second kick landed with a sickening thud, but, curiously, the Mortian didn't flinch and exhibited no sign of pain whatsoever.

Aiming his weapon at the desk, the other man, shorter and chunkier, motioned for casimir2 to move away. Another blast of laser vaporised some dials and instruments on the control panel. "Move this way! Both of you!" he ordered, indicating the oval doorway.

Aysha was the first to recover her composure. "What's 'appenin'? Tell me!" she demanded. "Who are you? What's goin' on?"

The taller man waited for a few seconds while his accomplice ushered the two Mortians through the doorway. "We don't want any trouble out of you two," he said, nodding towards us. "Just stay here out of the way until we get back."

Before either of us could respond, all four of them were gone, leaving us alone, as startled and bewildered as a pair of blind people at a busy intersection.

Aysha turned to me with an expression of sheer disbelief. "What the 'ell?" she cried. "Who are *they*? The ones wiv the guns. They're like us, right? From Earth?"

"Uh, well yes, kind of," I agreed. "Humans. From Earth. Just like you and me." I explained that when my grandmother had first arrived on the planet, the Mortian leader had assumed she would miss the society of her own species, so he had arranged for the abduction of a dozen young adults from various prisons near her home back on Earth (he had figured that their incarceration had rendered them expendable). So, anyway, unless there had been more recent abductees, the two guys with the laser weapons were presumably descended from those prisoners.

"Well, I'm *so* reportin' them!" Aysha managed to force a smile.

One thing was clear. Not only was there going to be no welcome reception for us, but apparently, there was not even going to be any coffee. Nothing. No coffee. Just some kind of crazy ambush. No streamers and no coffee. Also… and my brain was trying to avoid processing this… but when that laser beam had demolished the instruments on casimir2's desk, did that put paid to our prospects of ever…? No! No, surely not. Perish the thought!

I needed a coffee.

Like most people, I guess, I like to swim in the mysteries of life until I'm completely soaked. Then I like to dry off in the warm glow of something perfectly banal, comforting and obvious. If you hang around in the mysteries for too long, you can get all pruned and wrinkly.

Oh god, I needed a coffee.

NO PLACE LIKE HOME

Apparently, Aysha and I weren't the only ones who were struggling to fathom the unfathomable events that had unfolded since our arrival. To say things had also been turned upside down for yukawa3 is an understatement worthy of a Nobel Prize for Understatement.

In an effort to avoid confusion in the chronology of events, I'm going to tell you what happened to yukawa3 and casimir2 after they were escorted away from us, even though I didn't learn any of this until later during a conversation with casimir2.

Firstly, I should acknowledge that I might have relied too heavily on casimir2's version of events. With the benefit of hindsight, I could and maybe should have been a bit more circumspect. Okay, I should have been as wary as a blind horse negotiating a revolving door in the dark, but at the time I had absolutely no reason to doubt his narrative. Forgive me if I've also embellished it slightly here and there (casimir2 was such a dour and uninteresting raconteur). So, whatever. This, anyway, in as much detail as I can remember, is casimir2's account of what happened when he and yukawa3 were escorted out of the wormhole control centre.

During the frenzied conversation Aysha and I had witnessed on our arrival, he (casimir2) had been trying, with only limited success, to explain to yukawa3 that the descendants of the earthling prison abductees had overpowered their android guards and broken out of their enclosure close to the vast methane lake known as nefeshchaya.

The nefeshchaya compound was effectively a colossal greenhouse with a closed earth-like ecosystem. It comprised a cluster of dwelling pods, some dairy animals, a food processing facility, an ice house and a variety of equipment, tools, machinery and materials plundered from farms and factories on Earth. The Mortians, unfailingly benevolent and protective, had bent over backwards, providing sophisticated water extraction kits, a fully sustainable sanitation system, some goldfish, a few MP3 players and a regular supply of cheesy puffs.

When the first generation of abductees had arrived in the early part of the twenty-first century, it had been decided that they should undergo heart surgery, even though the nefeshchaya ecosystem eliminated the need for blue blood cells. These heart mutations, however, were obviously not passed on to the next generation and the Mortians decided against further surgical interventions.

Neither the original abductees nor any of their descendants had been inclined to perceive nefeshchaya as any kind of utopia. Having been wrenched from their home planet in such preposterous circumstances, the former Earth dwellers had seethed with resentment. And with each successive generation, the deep hostility they all harboured towards their Mortian guardians had just grown deeper and deeper.

So, having wrested control of the nefeshchaya boundary, the captives had turned captors, rounding up the entire Mortian population (all thirty of them) with the exception of yukawa3, who had been in transit from Earth (accompanying Aysha and myself), and casimir2, who had been engaged in securing his (and our) safe passage. Once they'd been rounded up, they were all gathered together in a bar room in the nefeshchaya complex.

You're probably wondering why the population of Melinda was so tiny. The Mortians' explanation was simple: they had evolved exponentially and had spent eons creating a fair and equitable state where every inhabitant had been scrupulously engineered to fulfil a specific role in society. Once all the roles had been allocated, no subsequent expansion was deemed either necessary or desirable, since any further population increase would have been redundant in terms of their needs as a species. Well, that, at any rate, is *my* interpretation of the official Mortian doctrine. They genuinely believed they had contrived a quintessence of civilisation whereby no one ever got marginalised, there were never any sources of conflict and the planet flourished like a summer harvest as a result. Since everything was so perfect and since they enjoyed long, healthy, disease-free lives, reproduction was carried out infrequently on a one-out, one-in basis, so the net population remained the same. And no, I don't mean the female devoured the male immediately after coitus. For one thing, the Mortians were asexual and for another thing, that would be just gross. If one of the thirty died, he or she (they were actually monomorphic or polymorphic or something like that – I could never really figure it out) was replaced by a clone by means of a genetic engineering process. Maybe there was some kind of assignation in a petri dish - I don't know the science exactly. Anyway, there was none of that unmatched chromosome and sexual procreation business we're familiar with on Earth. But, once subjected to even preliminary scrutiny, even *this* feature of Mortian civilisation fell apart like a dried seed pod. Why, for example, had my grandmother been mooted as a successor to the planetary leader if a replacement could have been cloned? And, furthermore, why was polkingbeal67 subsequently promoted to that role? I wondered if replacements for both the leader and smolin9 *had* indeed been cloned, because, as far as I was aware, the population of thirty had not reduced. These were questions to which I was keen to get answers during my time on the planet.

Anyway, convinced that they had reached an evolutionary plateau, the thirty Mortians saw themselves as paragons of enlightenment. I have since discovered the full extent of their self-delusional bubble. All the grandiose schemes they had concocted to fashion their world according to their academic fantasies had been nothing more than an exercise in developing a superiority complex. Over the course of time, I heard *all* of their transformational claims, from intergalactic justice to the brotherhood of indigenous peoples. But as soon as they were exposed to even the flimsiest wisp of empirical evidence, those claims disappeared like chillok ninjas during a triple eclipse on Omega Kasan (sorry, but this, according to my grandmother, had been one of smolin9's favourite analogies).

The Mortians had always been fond of repeating a certain proverb to admonish civilisations they considered to be too belligerent: 'when two goopmutts fight, the grass suffers.' Well, the grass on planet Melinda must have suffered a great deal! And it must have suffered without any blame being attributable to the much-maligned goopmutts, because, in actual fact, the Mortians had waged an endless succession of internal and foreign wars that had decimated the population to the point where they barely qualified as a credible species under the terms of the Intergalactic Charter! Hey, it's even worse than that. Most Mortians insisted that intervention was always and everywhere wrong in principle. They boasted of the great pains they took to avoid foreign entanglements of all kinds. But the truth is, as I discovered in due course, their *other* principles led to them engaging in *more* intergalactic conflicts than any other peoples in the known universe, with the possible exceptions of the chilloks and the so-called Liberators of Trox.

It might seem improbable that the Mortians should harbour such imperial ambitions, given the limitations of their population, but there *have* been parallels on Earth. Back as far as the middle of the twentieth century, a few guerrillas overcame a French army that boasted an overwhelming numerical, technological, military and economic advantage in the Algerian War of Independence. The North Vietnamese inflicted a similarly unlikely defeat on the American superpower a decade or so later. They prevailed because they learned how to turn a local dispute into a global campaign and how to harness public opinion to their cause (even in the countries whose governments they were fighting against).

As far as I could tell, the Mortians revelled in the moral certainty that all collateral destruction was justified in the name of ideological progress. Incapable of seeing other life forms as being as important as their own, they pursued a ruthlessly self-aggrandising aspiration to impose their own particular brand of civilisation. They were oblivious to the misery they inflicted on others and heedless of the intrinsic value of interdependent species and heterogeneous worlds.

It might be tempting to ridicule their fatuous self-deception, but I think it behoves those of us from Earth to keep shtum and exercise a little discretion, because, until fairly recently, we believed that the Earth was the centre of the universe. We also thought that our planet was flat and that God had created the world in six days. Furthermore, we abused and persecuted all those who denied this consensus. So, yeah, I think we'll cut them a little slack. Furthermore, it's probably the case that over the centuries the vast majority of empires on Earth had been founded on blood. Their power had been imposed and maintained through oppression and war. And, if you think about it, the imperial elites justified it by believing they were, like missionaries, magnanimously offering their superior culture to the people they conquered.

Why would the Mortians be any different?

I think I've digressed a little, don't you? Actually, let's be honest – I've been digressing like a giraffe on ice! So, where was I? Ah yes, well, when our safe arrival from Earth had been secured, two of the nefeshchayan earthlings were dispatched by cruiser to pick us all up from the wormhole control centre. As you know, they actually only picked up casimir2 and yukawa3, but their original remit had been to capture all *four* of us - the two Mortians (casimir2 and yukawa3) along with me and Aysha. And they were supposed to have conveyed all of us to nefeshchaya as quickly as possible, since any delay might jeopardise their (the nefeshchayans') health. Their vulnerability due to lack of blue blood cells could only be tolerated for short periods of time - extended absences from the special nefeshchaya ecosystem risked causing dysfunction. Anyway, the plan was changed because a serious issue had arisen. Try as they might, the earthlings had failed to persuade the Mortians to perform the necessary medical interventions on Aysha and myself, so we were to be left in the wormhole control centre pending a resolution to the dispute. Apparently, the necessary medical equipment was only available in the control centre.

As for the Mortians, well, casimir2 warned yukawa3 that there were other issues besides the earthling insurgency. One of them, in casimir2's opinion, was the Mortian leader's wild and demented state of mind. Incensed by his incarceration and convinced that earthlings were the source of all his problems, polkingbeal67 had allegedly been threatening to hang yukawa3 upside down from the nearest upside-down invercresco tree for the heinous crime of introducing two *more* earthlings to the planet.

On arrival at nefeshchaya, yukawa3 was greeted by polkingbeal67 with a howl of blood-curdling fury followed by a volley of abuse followed by a frenzied attempt at strangulation with a piece of seaweed, which the hapless victim only escaped by feigning death.

"Good to see you," said polkingbeal67, recovering his composure in a remarkably sudden transformation. Round his neck was an absurdly ostentatious necklace of long lozenge-shaped crystals. "Good trip?"

Yukawa3 flinched, expecting his head to part company with the rest of his body. "Yeh, thank you," he ventured tentatively, "but, verily, there's no place like home. I hope that answers your question."

"So, you've brought two more earthlings to visit us." The planetary leader's inflection suggested it wasn't a question.

Yukawa3 peered at polkingbeal67 with big eyes, as if he was begging for mercy. He started to speak and then stopped himself. Then he gulped.

One forefinger tapping meditatively at his eye patch, polkingbeal67 sat himself heavily into a large, brown leather armchair. "I don't understand you," he said. "Why do you do these things? You worry me. Nothing about you makes any sense. Why are you always looking for trouble? Tell me what you want."

"What I want?"

"Yes," said polkingbeal67, peering intently, his forehead puckered in apparent concentration. "What do you *want*? What makes you tick? What is it you really want out of life? Tell me, what do you want to be when you grow up?"

Yukawa3 thought for a moment. "Verily, I'd quite like my own TV game-show. Or maybe go on the talk show circuit," he said. "Wait, I *am* grown up!"

With all the sincerity of a TV game-show host, polkingbeal67 squinted his eyes and laughed.

Louder and louder. The crystal necklace shook violently. He was like the laughing chandelier! Casimir2 does not get the credit (or blame) for that remark.

Before too long, the laugh morphed into a menacing cackle. "I am still your leader," he declared, examining his reflection in a mirror. "Listen to me!"

Yukawa3 and the rest of the Mortian population gathered in a loose huddle in front of their imposing ruler, nodding in dutiful assent.

Polkingbeal67's latest accessory from Earth was a yellow and navy golf umbrella. He twirled it with one hand and then closed it with a decisive snap. "Are there any among you who oppose my rule?" he asked in a tone that sounded calm and benevolent.

"Permission to speak?" asked yukawa3.

Polkingbeal67 cocked his head to one side and adjusted his eye patch. "Permission granted."

"You're behaving like a total dork!" said yukawa3 with all the confidence that comes with knowing full well that the leader would have absolutely no knowledge of the pejorative earthling term. And then, as an afterthought, he added, "Sir."

"Thank you," said polkingbeal67, still projecting an

air of casual solemnity. "And I can reassure you that you may rely on me to continue being a dork to all of you during this crisis. I will be both a dork and a pillar of strength and together we will turn this situation around. We will beat this. Wait, what exactly is a dork? Is it like a synonym for a heroic overlord?"

With no trace of a smirk on his face, yukawa3 simply nodded and said, "Uh huh. A complete dork." Again, he added "sir" as an afterthought. Then becoming serious, he went on, "We've got to do something about the earthlings, Neil and Aysha. If we leave them much longer, the lack of blue blood cells will compromise their metabolism and some of their organs may start to fail. And if you think that sounds alarmist, well, it is."

Polkingbeal67 stared at the dark hardwood floor. The room had been designed to mimic a traditional Irish bar. Dark wood panelling ran along the lower half of the walls. The top half boasted decorative shamrocks and Celtic crosses. Behind polkingbeal67's chair was a shelf displaying horseshoes and other Irish memorabilia. Signs with neon lights completed the reproduction. "Why should I care about those infernal earthlings?" he mumbled, looking up again and ostentatiously opening his umbrella.

"Neil is Melinda's grandson," yukawa3 pointed out. "Remember Melinda? The woman after whom this planet has been named? The woman you gave your heart to?" Realising the comic ambiguity of his words, he stammered, "I mean literally, not, y'know... not figuratively, like... as in any romantic context."

Polkingbeal67 stood up and made a stabbing motion with the umbrella. "All the more reason to leave them to their fate," he responded in a surly tone.

"We can't just let them die!" yukawa3 protested. "That's barbaric! That would be a flagrant breach of intergalactic treaty stuff or... I don't know, whatever! I wouldn't do that if I was you. Come on, you're not as preposterous as I look. As a planetary leader, you cannot stoop that low."

If polkingbeal67 had had earthling eyebrows he would have been arching them disdainfully. "So, how low am I allowed to stoop?" he asked rhetorically, before losing his patience. "Oh, do spare me the melodrama," he drawled, before commencing to pace the room like a caged animal, perhaps an angry gorilla, certainly an animal that could brandish an umbrella anyway. "You're a traitor!"

"I-I'm not a traitor," yukawa3 stammered. He racked his brains for a suitable riposte. As was always the case with the hapless yukawa3, the racking thing never produced anything except a stretched-out brain.

"I'm placing you under arrest, you crazy prokaryote!"

"But we're *all* under arrest," yukawa3 pointed out.

Polkingbeal67 was in front of the mirror now, hands on hips, jutting out his chin in what he imagined was a heroic pose. "Arrest him!" he commanded no one in particular. When a flunky jumped forward and seized yukawa3 by the arm, he added, "Don't let him out of your sight!" Turning to casimir2, he said, "Go and get the attention of one of those snake earthlings! I want you to pretend you're going to perform the blood cell procedure on the two new arrivals. But, listen to me - you're *actually* going to send them back to Earth!"

Casimir2 advised him that the nefeshchayan insurgents had zapped the portal controls and that he didn't know how much functionality was left.

Polkingbeal67 jabbed the umbrella at the back of a chair causing it to crash to the floor. "Well, find out!" he said tersely. His uncovered eye flashed for a moment, and then he prodded casimir2 in the ribs with the brolly. More than once, apparently.

And so concludes casimir2's account of yukawa3's reunion with his fellow Mortians.

WHERE ARE THE TOILETS?

Tic Tacs and ketchup go together like me and Neil Armstrong went to the moon together. We didn't and they don't. But a small container of Tic Tacs and a sachet of tomato ketchup were the sum total of edible items Aysha and I discovered during a thorough search of the magma chamber and all our pockets. Well, to be fair, there were also a few vials of HDA. But there's edible and there's edible and HDA is about as edible as liquidised skunk.

So, there we were, ensnared in a bizarre situation we didn't understand, on a planet we didn't know anything about. And the thing that was really propelling itself to the top of my list of priorities was, well, it was… *where were the toilets?* We hadn't thought to ask. We'd been abandoned for at least two hours now and nature has a habit of calling when it's least convenient. I also really needed a wash, for reasons I may have hinted at earlier. And so, disoriented, discouraged and discombobulated, Aysha and I ventured forth, through the oval doorway, in search of answers to myriad questions about our place in the universe and, er, the location of the toilets. Imagine our frustration as our exploratory (and rather urgent) meander along the labyrinthine magma corridors led to, well, more magma corridors.

Wait. Why were there no signs to the exits? No, never mind that. Why were there no signs to the toilets? So, the corridors eventually led to rooms and the rooms eventually led to the precious porcelain privy. Well, as it happens, no porcelain. On this planet, the loos were inevitably constructed from magma. These were auto-sanitising loos and the waste matter was immediately converted and expelled in the form of tiny spherical capsules of something I assumed to be biogas. I breathed a sigh of relief. At last my brain could focus properly. Clarity was restored. That should have been a good thing, right? Unfortunately, no, it served only to put me in a blind panic as I realised something that had not occurred to me until now - namely that if my grandmother had needed heart surgery to survive on the planet, then it stood to reason that Aysha would require this too. Oh yes, and so would I.

I felt strangely calm in the face of that dreadful realisation and I resolved to wait for the right moment to break it to Aysha. No, okay, you probably guessed - I blurted it out straight away: "Oh my God, Aysha!" I exclaimed with all the composure of a mixed bag of mice and cats. "We've gotta have heart surgery!"

Aysha's facial expressions cycled from dismay to bewilderment and back again as I explained the ramifications. One particular ramification caused her eyes to pop out on stalks like a cartoon character (and I could almost hear a klaxon sound effect)! "Wait," she said, "So, what you're sayin' is this - if we 'ave this surgery, we can't go back 'ome?"

We looked around for somewhere to sit and reflect. Clustered points of crimson light spun slowly and soothingly around us as we walked. After a while, we perched ourselves on a ledge in one of the many jaw-droppingly beautiful chambers we had encountered during our search for the toilets. We'd already seen walls that boasted all the colours of the rainbow, but in this particular chamber the predominant hues were blue and orange. There were columns and arches and pilasters and sculptures of what were presumably illustrious figures of Mortian history. The ceiling was embellished with niches of white magma, polished smooth like marble. The mood was right, so I proceeded to reassure Aysha, employing all my customary charm and tact. Okay, I'll own up, I just stared disconsolately at the magma walls and I was about as reassuring as a brain surgeon with an instruction manual.

In all probability, the entire complex, with its twisting maze of corridors and chambers, had been formed by volcanic activity thousands of years ago when molten rock had forced its way through the planet's crust. Subsequently, it had been transformed wall by wall, chamber by chamber, into the architectural masterpiece that our eyes now beheld.

"It's enchanting though, isn't it?" I mused, in a pathetic attempt to change the subject. Bathed in a pale blur of blue and orange light, none of this seemed to be the nightmare it actually was. "I suppose this whole facility is under the ground."

Aysha fixed me with an empty stare resembling that of a Rottweiler with toothache. "Just as well," she snarled, "because no one will hear your screams when I tear you limb from flamin' limb! Seriously? Are you jus' gonna prattle on about the décor?" She seemed uncharacteristically hostile, and I wondered if the wormhole trip had affected her mood a little, or, indeed, if it had totally transmogrified her DNA. Wagging a finger at me, she looked as if she was about to go off the deep end. And then her rant stopped abruptly. She was trembling, and I'll never forget the look in her eyes. Were we about to get a Jane Austen or a Charlotte Bronte moment? Taking hold of my arms, she clutched me passionately (okay, it could have been savagely). I braced myself as she spoke falteringly (I guess the faltering thing could have been voice-quavering, lower-lip-trembling emotional fervour, but, to be honest, it could also have been incandescent rage): "I don' know 'ow to put this," she mumbled, an apologetic inflection of voice unmistakable (well, apologetic, infuriated, whatever). "I know I came 'ere wiv you voluntarily, and I know it's gonna be really tough for you cos you wanted to be a peace ambassador for Earth, an' you wanted to honour your grandma's legacy by fosterin' good relations an' all, but -" She hesitated as a wave of emotion washed over her. The impact of what she was saying was clearly affecting her now (or, I have to admit, she could have just been preparing to hammer home her point by punching me in the stomach). "This isn't what I thought I was signin' up for, Neil," she said emphatically, thumping the magma with her fist. "I'm *not* 'avin' any surgery! And we're goin' back 'ome straight away! You 'ear me? Get us back 'ome, Neil! We're goin' 'ome!" Fixing me with a particularly hard stare, she added "Now!"

So, Jane Austen or Charlotte Bronte, thug-style. Several seconds passed. I didn't dare to turn and meet her eyes.

'Houston, we have a problem', I thought to myself.

ENCOUNTER WITH A BLANID

First, let me explain something. Aysha and I shared a strong emotional bond. A platonic one, but a strong one. People have sensuality and spirituality. And there is a highly dynamic and complex array of psycho-social phenomena in the landscape of human interplay. Some of it's rather base, some much loftier. I'm not sure exactly where Aysha and I connected, but it was definitely towards the non-sexual end of the array. When we first met, we were like two doves that had also never met. No, that's not right. I suppose we were more like a sparrow and a greenfinch. We were like two streams that ran alongside one another, never merging or crossing. Oh, wait, I suppose that's not a very good analogy, because it doesn't allow for the possibility of a flood. Well, whatever. I'm sure you know what I mean. And, anyway, there hadn't been a flood.

So, Aysha was pacing up and down, shooting me the occasional withering glare and sighing irritably at nothing in particular and everything in general.

You know what? I wasn't cut out for this. None of it - space travel, being friends with people to the point where you have to take responsibility for what happens to them, knowing what to do in adverse circumstances. None of it. My dad used to say there's no wall so high and no river so wide that you can't just go home and eat pizza. Well, he was wrong. I sat staring at the floor with a scowl like a dark horseshoe embedded in my forehead.

It makes no difference whether it's serious or popular, high or low, our culture abounds with examples of people who thrive on adversity – people who know exactly what to do and when to do it. They proliferate in our history books and they swarm all over our newspapers and TV screens. Listen, don't they have any idea how *annoying* they are? As for me, when life gives me lemons, I squeeze them. And the juice stings my eyes like hell.

At that moment, I was fretting like crazy about what could have happened to yukawa3 and casimir2. I was fretting about Aysha's outburst. Obviously, I was fretting about the damage inflicted on the control desk that appeared to configure the wormhole portal. In particular, I was fretting about the way yukawa3 had conducted himself throughout the whole thing. Having enticed us to travel here with him on the premise of intergalactic cooperation, surely it was incumbent on him to ensure our safety and welfare, plus coffee, plus directions to the toilet facilities? Ashamed of myself, bitterly frustrated at my failure to exercise any control over events, I just sat, numb with misery, staring at distorted reflections in the polished magma.

If I'm honest, the thing that was now beginning to bother me more than anything else was the sudden malice in Aysha's demeanour.

When she had volunteered to accompany me on the trip, I had seen it as a clear sign that our friendship had deepened. What was it she'd said to me? Well, how could I forget? The whole moment was still crystal clear in my mind. Back in my apartment in Nuneaton, yukawa3 had just announced that the chilloks had abandoned their attempt to invade Earth. Wait, I should explain that yukawa3's mission had been to warn us all that these chillok creatures (I think I mentioned them to you before) had been bent on overthrowing humankind and had been surreptitiously invading the planet. So, anyway, after all this had got resolved, he had asked me to return with him to Smolin9 (or Melinda, as it is now known) to act as an ambassador, a go-between to bring about peace between our two planets. Well, basically, he wanted me to make his planet's leader see sense. The famously hawkish polkingbeal67 had declared war on Earth because his donated heart had been cremated along with the rest of my grandmother. The coordinates for the wormhole trip had been processed, and I had been obliged to accept or decline the invitation right there and then, with absolutely no opportunity to consult anyone. We had all been standing there - me, yukawa3, Aysha and a mutual friend called Disney – and you could have heard a pin drop. Finally, Aysha had gently clutched my arm and whispered, "You're not going without me!" The hairs on the back of my neck had stood up and I'd figured the two of us had just made a deep emotional and spiritual connection and... yes, well, I can't think of a time when my heart had felt so full.

But here, right now, I couldn't raise *any* feeling in my heart at all. Becoming increasingly despondent and miserable, I started wondering if a full heart actually weighed more than an empty one. Yes, honestly, that's what was going through my mind. You see, people always accused me of overthinking, but I had never really been smart enough to overthink things. *Under*thinking was my trademark. Do you sometimes wonder if you're a head, heart or hands kind of person? I do. Everyone, it seems, is ruled by one of them – or maybe a combination of them. At that point, I began to contemplate the notion that I might like to be ruled, for a limited period of time, by my left knee, simply because the head, heart and hands have been monopolising things for long enough.

Hell, that was enough! I decided I should definitely get up and *do* something. Anything.

"Wait here," I told Aysha. "I'm going to find someone."

And so I started wandering in and out of chambers and passages (and focus and emotional states). Some of the smaller chambers had frescoed ceilings. Sections of the walls were tapestried and the air was heavy with a musty smell. The larger rooms were similar but more sparsely furnished, and the ceilings and walls were less colourful, apart from the ubiquitous clusters of red light. Some of them contained nothing but long tables flanked with exquisitely carved chairs. None of them offered any solace or diversion. Or people. After a while, one compartment became virtually indistinguishable from the next. Ultimately, they all seemed to coalesce into a single amorphous structure.

Suddenly, the blurriness evaporated and I found myself outside in the open air. Standing in a sort of cloistered quadrangle, I gazed up at a clear azure sky, illuminated by two suns. Yukawa3 had told me that the composition of the planet's atmosphere was broadly similar to that of Earth, except that it was richer in certain reducing gases, especially methane. It smelled like rotting vegetables and made breathing just a little bit difficult. In the centre of the quadrangle stood a sprawling, apparently inverted tree, tangled root-like branches clawing beseechingly at the sky. It created a threadbare canopy of shade that provided scant reprieve from the searing heat. Scattered haphazardly on the ground, large green pods or husks, presumably the fruit of the tree, lay around in various states of decay. Beyond the tree, a broad expanse of gently undulating plains, broken here and there with scrub and rocky outcrops and clusters of what I assumed must be habitation pods, stretched away to the horizon. At this point, I realised that although the surface gravity was remarkably similar to the Earth's, it was maybe a bit weaker, so I experimented with a few bunny hops like Gene Cernan on the moon during the Apollo 17 mission…

A small reptilian creature ran out from a crevice and looked up at me with green jade eyes.

"I come in peace," I muttered tentatively. Too late. Unleashing a cloud of what I soon realised was poisonous venom, it wriggled sinuously away behind the tree. I was standing at least ten feet away, but fine particles immediately reached my lungs. Coughing, spluttering and feeling nauseous, I turned to go back inside, but everything started spinning. I fell to my knees and my insides twisted violently, causing me to roll over and vomit (again).

POINT OF NO RETURN

When I finally came to, I had a kind of hangover like I'd been kicked in the head by a pantomime horse wearing army boots. I say 'pantomime' because someone was shouting "It's behind you!" I was slumped in a padded chair, and on the table behind me was a vial of blue-green swirly liquid. No cherry. No parasol. A man's tanned and freckled hand seized it and thrust it towards my face. "Take it!" The voice and the hand belonged to one of the nefeshchayans Aysha and I had encountered earlier, a mean-looking man named Ollie. "It's antivenom," he said. "You've been poisoned by a blanid. Down the 'atch! Then you'll be okay."

Staring at the swirling concoction, I recoiled slightly. I was not sure I could summon the energy to take the glass and lift it to my lips, but I managed it somehow. Noticing for the first time that the liquid emitted a weird, fluorescent glow, I shut my eyes tight and drank it down in one go. It fizzed slightly and tasted sour, but within seconds the tingling sensations in my limbs started to recede and my eyes cleared.

Looking around, I realised we were in the

wormhole control chamber in which we had first arrived. And I noticed there were three of us in the room – me, Ollie and casimir2, who was staring disconsolately at the mangled controls.

"Where's Aysha?" I asked.

"Listen, mate," said Ollie, who still had a mean look about him, the kind you get from being, you know, mean. "Take it easy. We don't know 'ow long you were lyin' there before we found you."

Casimir2 made a thin, high-pitched sound like a mouse with its tail caught in a trap. "Oh no! Oh noooooo!" he wailed in a curiously emotive voice, reminiscent of (and about as convincing as) a female opera singer being stabbed to death in the middle of an aria. "This… this isn't good. I've made a full inspection. Although the exit interface is viable per se, all the entry and re-entry controls are functional for voice communication only."

"I told you, didn't I?" said Ollie. "I zapped the controls for *incoming* transport."

I sat upright and turned to Ollie. "Where's Aysha?" I asked again, more urgently.

For the first time, I noticed a glimmer of sensitivity in his deep-set eyes. The jaw was still set hard, but the bottom lip twitched slightly. "She's gone," he said.

"Gone?" I echoed.

"Back to Earth," he said, touching his chin nervously. "She's gone back to Earth."

Weakened by the effects of not only the blanid poison but also the debilitating impact of blue blood cell deficiency, I was in no state to query what was happening, beyond vaguely trying to process the enormity of Aysha's sudden disappearance.

Ollie pointed to a small gold necklace lying on a magma shelf. "She left it."

Why would she leave the necklace? And why would she return to Earth? Without me? Why would she do that? Should I go after her? I like to think I usually have a mind like a steel trap, but at that moment it was like a steel trap that had been confiscated by animal rights activists and stashed away in a musty cupboard. And it was going rusty. I just *couldn't* process any of this. Turning to casimir2 for help and guidance, I could only manage a long, drawn out "Whaa…" before the anaesthetic took effect. As I drifted into semi-consciousness, I realised I had been administered something else, not just an antivenom potion.

Later, as I came round on a portable treatment table,

I became aware of the autosurgery android turning away from me. I felt uncomfortable and weak, but the physical effects were as nothing to the realisation that quickly dawned on me – without me having signed any kind of consent form, someone had performed the blue blood cell surgical procedure on me! I was stuck on Melinda for the rest of my days. I could never return to Earth and it was extremely unlikely that Aysha and I would ever see one another again. Immediately, my consciousness sought out the dark corners of my mind and I plunged into a depression that threatened to consume me. With all the clarity of a decades-old neglected fish tank, I staggered to my feet and said, "I woosh… I wash to appeal to some independent tribunal panel people and I woosh to claim condensation under breach of the Confection of Human Rights."

I guess it was at this point that casimir2, unbidden, took it upon himself to ignore me completely and deliver his lowdown on events that had occurred in nefeshchaya while Aysha and I had been left in the control centre complex. I don't know how much of what he told me really happened. I don't know how much of it I subconsciously chiselled and shaped later, or how much of it was chiselled and shaped by casimir2 before it even reached my ears. To be honest, I don't even know how much I cared at the time. What I *do* know is that, at that point, all my perceptions were as random as tumbleweed drifting haphazardly across a desert plain. However, I distinctly remember casimir2 examining his chest area and wincing. He told me that if I had been labouring under the misapprehension that polkingbeal67's umbrella was a metaphor for protection, I had better come up with some new apprehensions. And metaphors.

I'm not sure why he had felt inclined to tell me all this stuff. Obviously, I needed to be aware of the insurgency, but the rest of it seemed to me to have about as much relevance as a half-eaten tuna sandwich lying on a bench in a railway station back in Nuneaton. Perhaps, for some reason, he sought to poison my mind against polkingbeal67. Anyway, when he was finished, he wandered off into a corner and became preoccupied with his microwocky. Ollie took me aside to regale me with more details of what had happened to Aysha. Apparently, while I had been unconscious and disengaged from everything, Ollie had escorted casimir2 to the wormhole control centre complex with a remit to ensure that both Aysha and I underwent the necessary medical treatment to facilitate our survival on planet Melinda. I didn't comprehend why, at that moment, but, apparently, Aysha and I represented a very useful asset to the nefeshchaya earthlings.

Having discovered Aysha wandering aimlessly along the passageways, the pair had escorted her to the wormhole portal chamber and Ollie had made the mistake of leaving her alone with the Mortian while he set off to fetch a treatment table and an autosurgery android. He'd only been gone a couple of minutes, but it had proved long enough for the Mortian to configure and surreptitiously open the wormhole portal... and Aysha had been dispatched back to Earth.

Exasperated and incensed, Ollie had then proceeded to remind casimir2 of his obligations as a prisoner. This reminder took the form of several blows to the top of his head. Blessed with the agility of a kind of humanoid fish, casimir2 had apparently managed to evade most of the punches by wriggling and twisting himself out of trouble. He had also managed to retaliate by inflicting a few slaps of his own. When both had exhausted themselves, casimir2 had protested that Aysha's departure had been in accordance with the express wishes of the planetary leader, a protest that had elicited a few more instructive blows on the top of his head.

Just as I was starting to think about the tuna sandwich once again, casimir2 put down his microwocky and interrupted us. "We've got to go before Ollie here gets taken ill."

Evidently the pair of them had eventually calmed down and decided that compromise was the key to resolving their conflict. Ollie had doubtless figured that when damage limitation is the only show in town, you scramble for tickets. Having taken stock of the situation, his next course of action had become eminently clear. At that point, Aysha had been returned to Earth and could not be retrieved, but casimir2 had not managed to eject *both* of us. Once they'd found me and carried out the medical procedure, they could both claim to have carried out half of their respective missions.

The three of us, casimir2, Ollie and I, made our way out of the wormhole control centre, squeezed into an astonishing gull-wing hovercruiser and made our way to the nefeshchaya compound.

THE PUNCTURED BALL

I remember very little of the hovercruiser trip or my interrogation at the hands of the nefeshchayans, who were desperate to know what life on Earth was really like. My responses must have been inadequate and unimpressive, because they soon lost interest in me and left me to my own devices. Disconsolate and weary, I didn't know what to do with myself and spent several hours just wandering aimlessly around the compound, lamenting my sad fate. I was seriously hoping that all of this was some kind of hallucinatory aberration. Real soon, I figured, the bizarre fabrications of my imagination would be blown apart and scattered into oblivion by the total lack of objective sensory input. Opening my eyes wider, I stared and stared at an upside-down invercresco tree and laughed at its appearance. I mean, what the hell was it doing there in my primary visual cortex? Why didn't I just imagine something else? If I set my mind to it, I could have visualised a penguin climbing that tree, wearing sunglasses and a tutu, while the clouds above started singing 'Sweet Georgia Brown' …

At this point, Ollie came out and spoke to me. "You okay?" he asked. I nodded, unable to say anything that would really cover how I felt. I think he asked me if Aysha was my wife and I think for some reason I replied that she was. "Tough break," he said, not sounding particularly sympathetic. "Tough break."

"I'm okay," I lied. There was no sense trying to explain it to him. I couldn't understand it myself, let alone communicate it in words.

We were in a kind of neglected yard. Incongruous and strangely distressing, a pair of shoes straddled the top of the border fence. The nefeshchaya Earth-like ecosystem was bounded by an invisible membrane, but, bizarrely, someone had seen fit to construct fences. For all the world, the shoes looked like they had become animated and were trying to escape. For obvious reasons, I could totally identify with the plight of that pair of shoes.

"So, what actually 'appened?" Ollie asked. "Were you abducted? I know you told us you came 'ere voluntarily, but, y'know, seriously? Hey, it's okay, I'm not grillin' you. I'm just a regular guy, y'know? We never did introductions back in the worm'ole control centre, did we? Your name's Neil, right? I'm Oliver. You can call me Ollie. You're gonna need a friend 'ere, buddy. So, tell me, did that Mortian guy, yukawa3, kidnap the pair of you?"

Still staring at the shoes, I shook my head. "No," I

said, "he really didn't. He came to Earth to warn us about an invasion."

"An invasion?"

"Yeah, there's a weird species evolved from ants. And apparently they …"

"The chilloks?"

"Yes," I confirmed, slightly bamboozled. "The chilloks. You know about them? You know about the chilloks?"

"Of course I do. They tried to invade *this* planet too," Ollie pointed out. "Some time back. Before I was born."

Obviously, I was aware of this and, obviously, I suppose I shouldn't have been surprised that the descendants of my grandmother's peers were familiar with the story. I was about to tell him about my grandmother, but he interrupted me. "Wanna coffee, Neil?" he asked.

I shook my head. "No thanks, Ollie. I think maybe I should just lie down somewhere. Is that possible? I feel very tired."

"Nice cup o' coffee would wake you up."

"No," I mumbled distractedly. "I've always found

the best way to cure tiredness is to sleep it off. A nice cup of *sleep* is what I *want*," I replied.

"A cup of *what*?"

"Sleep," I said.

"Sleep?"

"Uh huh."

"Huh?"

"Uh huh, yeah."

I don't suppose it was a conversation either of us was particularly proud of. Taking the opportunity to sort out a few domestic issues, I quizzed him about where I might find a comfortable bed and how I might get hold of a toothbrush – I hadn't packed one – and was there any way I could get a haircut – it had become a little unkempt and boasted a few crop circles?

A breath of wind, possibly the first I had been aware of since my arrival, ruffled the long quiff of hair at the front of Ollie's otherwise closely-cropped head. Looking up, I noticed clouds forming in spiral patterns against a backdrop of a deep blue sky that was now assuming a faint greenish tinge.

As we walked, we passed an improvised basketball

hoop attached to a pole. Ollie picked up a punctured basketball. Where had they got that from? Assuming he was going to start shooting baskets, I stopped to watch him.

"Tell me 'bout England, Neil," Ollie insisted, wiping his nose with the back of his hand. "Is it still called England? Is there still a queen? Or, y'know, a king? A royal family?"

"Ye-e-es," I said tentatively, wary of being subjected to another interrogation. I really didn't feel like being besieged with a whole slew of new questions about Earth. "It's still called England. But the monarchy was abolished a while back. It's not even a country as such any longer."

Ollie furrowed his brow and looked utterly perplexed. "Not a country? How is it not a country? You mean it's one of them republics?"

"No, it's not a country or a republic or any kind of nation-state."

He stared in astonishment bordering on dismay. "What *is* it then?"

"Well, I'll try to explain," I said, immediately regretting my words. "The planet is now pretty much a borderless world. There are no sovereign nation-states as such. Not any longer. You gotta remember, countries and nations are just abstract notions. They're not real things. People just created them in their collective imaginations."

"So, there are no governments?"

"No *national* governments."

Ollie squeezed the basketball with both hands, the expression on his face oscillating between wonder and distress. "No presidents or prime ministers?"

It was no good. I had been trapped into delivering a full treatise on how life on Earth had changed over the course of the last century. I pointed out that people on Earth now espoused global democracy and global governance, a World Parliament headed by an elected POW (President of the World). And I explained the move towards a free market ideology, unfettered migration and multiculturalism. Oblivious to his evident lack of comprehension, I kept talking without skipping a beat. Economic globalisation, I insisted, had created prosperity and opportunity for billions of people on Earth. It had proved to be hugely empowering and it had made the world safer and healthier too.

Ollie blinked at me with confused, disbelieving fish eyes and repeated his original question: "Not a country?" He chewed on his bottom lip in thought as I paused to let him process everything I was telling him, then he asked, "So, is it really better? Does it work?"

"To be honest with you," I said. "And bear in mind this may be just my own opinion. Once the borders disappeared, I guess what happened was that big business kinda took over." I scratched my head, unsure of how much to tell. "That's not how it was meant to be, of course."

"How was it *meant* to be?"

"Free market capitalism was supposed to benefit *everyone*."

"How?" Ollie asked, tossing the ball to me. "How does it compare with what we do 'ere? We all do our own individual jobs in nefeshchaya and we 'ave money and stuff, but we kinda run a cooperative... I mean, yeah, John is our 'igh commander, but 'e's like one of us really. We share things and we're all allowed to 'ave access to the chickens and camels and so on."

"We'd probably call that, er, camelism," I said, thinking of communism and getting distracted by the reference to camels. "Did you say camels?"

"Where do you think we get our milk from?" he replied. "Listen, your free market capitalism thing is basically people exploiting people. Isn't it? Our system isn't like that."

"No," I said, recalling a joke Aysha had told me once. "With *your* system, it's the other way round."

The joke pirouetted on its left foot and fell flat on its face. Ollie simply turned his baffled eyes towards me. "What if someone just wanted to be, y'know, 'onest and kind and loyal and 'ard-workin'?"

"Well," I answered, with a creeping sense of unease. "Those are valuable things, obviously. To some extent. Especially the hard-working thing. Where do you keep the camels?"

Ollie chewed his bottom lip, thinking it over. "So, with this free market capitalism thing, don't the best and brightest get to be richer an' more powerful than the rest? Exactly what's to stop the owners jus' gettin' richer and richer at ev'ryone else's expense?"

"Exactly," I said. "*Nothing* stops that happening. Not as such. I suppose it was all based on a belief in serendipity."

"Eh, do what?"

Defending one's home turf is a very basic instinct and, despite myself, I could feel it kicking in. "Serendipity," I repeated, passing the ball back to

Ollie. "You know? Believing good stuff will happen by accident - by means of an invisible hand, if you like. So, what happens is - people undercut their competitors by charging lower and lower prices. Obviously, they're *really* driven by self-interest and just want to maximise their profits…" The more I explained it, the less I understood it.

Ollie interrupted me with a cough. "But, wait, 'ow can they maximise their profits if they're cuttin' their prices?" he protested.

"Well, yeah," I said. "But it's not a race to the bottom. Actually, it's not a zero-sum game at all."

"Why not? It sounds like it. We've got a food shop 'ere. Lizzie's sister, Eva, runs it. And if we 'ad another one and they started undercutting one another's prices, surely it would be a competition that only one of 'em could win?"

"Well," I said. "You're assuming that the pie never gets any bigger."

"What pie? They'd make bigger pies?"

"No, I mean the overall economic pie," I clarified with all the clarity of a pocket-dial voicemail. "If the pie stays the same size, as I guess it does here, it doesn't matter how you slice it - some people might get richer, but only at the expense of other people.

Whereas on Earth, I guess we've kind of found a way of providing a bigger and bigger economic pie for everyone to benefit from."

"But does everyone get a fair slice?"

"Well," I demurred. "In theory – and this is where the serendipity thing comes in - distribution is achieved dynamically and automatically without having to impose egalitarian rules like the ones you people here presumably have to obey." I was starting to get irritated, like I was trying to defend the indefensible. "But, actually, it doesn't quite work like that," I went on. "Economic success is based on an entrepreneurial dream in which the entrepreneurs are rewarded. That's how it works."

"So, if the entrepreneur people get greedy, that's good, is it?"

"Well, yeah," I said. "Because when the pie grows, everyone benefits." Then I started to see it from Ollie's perspective. What I was describing was a free market democracy that was clearly exploited by people who didn't want a *fair and equitable* society at all. Was that right?

Ollie made as if he was going to punch the ball, but he tossed it to me instead. "So, if Eva puts up 'er prices, everyone benefits? That can't be right."

"It depends on what she does with the increased profit," I explained. "If she invests the money in getting hold of better, tastier, healthier, more interesting food and devises more efficient ways of transporting it and storing it... And maybe hires an assistant to help with the increased customer demand…"

"So, she reinvests the profit in 'er business…"

"Yes."

"Which brings about *more* profit?"

"Yes."

Letting out a sigh, Ollie shook his head and stared at the ground. "But, no," he protested. "We only have so much money and we can only eat so much food."

I dropped the ball, but it bounced just like a bag of mashed potato doesn't bounce. "Well, what if someone else sets up a shop, specialising in health foods?" I suggested rhetorically. "And then someone else starts up a bakery? So, then you've got some competition for people's money."

"'Ow would they do it? It would take a lot of 'ard work and money to start up a new shop."

"They would apply for credit," I said.

"Credit?"

"Yeah," I said, as Ollie picked up the ball. "So, they borrow money from someone - I don't know, maybe John, maybe friends and family, anyone who believes they'll make a success of it. And, eventually, these people get paid back with interest."

After I'd explained what interest was and how it worked, Ollie nodded in approval. "Okay," he said. "I think I'm gettin' the idea. So, if I were to set up a new shop in competition with Eva, do you think everyone would be okay with it?"

I laughed a little weakly. "Bit late now," I said. "I thought you wanted to leave here and settle on Earth? Anyway, I don't want to create the impression that it all works perfectly on Earth. It doesn't. It really doesn't. Free market capitalism is not a panacea. It often fails, owing to corruption, greed and self-serving culture."

"And what about camelism?"

"Camelism?"

"You said our system is called camelism."

The penny dropped. "Oh, yeah. Sorry, I meant to say communism."

"Nothin' to do with the camels?"

No," I confirmed. "Nothing to do with camels. But, seriously, you keep camels here? Large desert animals with humps?"

Ollie shook his head. "They don't have 'umps. But the milk's very good. So, what about camelism, communism, whatever you called it?"

"Yeah, well, communism fails too."

"Because of the pie thing?"

"Yeah, and, um, because of corruption, greed and self-serving culture." I said, disconcerted. "There's always a lot of political tension. Sometimes, even with free market capitalism, the pie actually *shrinks* because…" I fell silent for a moment as I considered my words. "Well, it shrinks because the reins of morality and ethics and the harness of redistribution sometimes just kind of restrain the hunger and perseverance of the entrepreneurs. Yes, so, from time to time, you get a world government that decides to impose heavy taxation on the wealth creators."

"Yeah," said Ollie. "My parents mentioned taxes. So, do you think if I opened a new shop, John would introduce taxes? What 'appens to the money the world government raises?"

"Well, for example, they might use it to pay out generous unemployment benefits. It's really popular with voters."

"But not with the people who are getting taxed, I guess?"

"Nope," I said. "The wealth creators think it would be far better if the government left the money with *them*. They reckon they would use it to start up new shops, businesses and factories, so they could actually *hire* the unemployed and there would be no need for benefits. But, anyway, right now, to all intents and purposes, global corporations pretty much rule the world - economically, politically, environmentally and culturally. Thing is, Ollie, you'd think that even the business classes might start to have second thoughts. No one wants telephone-number salaries in the boardroom on the one hand and people sleeping in shop doorways on the other. It tears the social fabric, y'know? So, you'd think some of them might aspire to forge a bit of social cohesion and cooperation, but, hey, how do you get people to cooperate when they want to be more successful than the next guy? No, you don't exactly get the fat cats calling for government intervention to protect people from market forces."

"Fat cats?" asked Ollie, blinking again, like an owl in bright daylight. "Now you're losin' me again."

"The key thing is this," I said. "Economic globalisation has been great, but political globalisation has become a disaster in recent times. All the decision-making has been pushed upwards and way beyond the reach of democratic checks and balances. Your ordinary person on Earth now has absolutely no stake in the really important decisions."

Ollie took one hand off the deformed basketball and fingered his chin. "So people don't 'ave anyone to represent them?"

"Well, that's it," I said. "There *are* politicians, but they're effectively proxies for global corporate interests."

"That's terrible, Neil! You'd think the people would've got angry about it. No? Don't they feel they should 'ave a stake in 'ow things work? What about things bein' fair and equitable?"

"Well, in theory there's equality of opportunity. Not much equality of outcome, if I'm honest. But, listen, people *aren't* equal really, are they? Everyone has their own different genetic code, and everyone's exposed to different environmental influences all through their lives. And, as far as globalism is concerned, well, the thing is… over the course of time, I guess people have kind of had their brains rewired." As Ollie stared blankly at me, a sardonic chuckle bubbled up in my throat. I'd been trying to keep the sarcasm out of my voice but I finally gave way. "Sorry, what I mean is, they've been persuaded of the virtues of having a world view as opposed to a more local one. And they've embraced globalism in all its forms. Meanwhile, the rich have become cocooned from ordinary people's ordeals."

"Terrible!" Ollie repeated. He lobbed the basketball and missed the hoop by several feet. "Just terrible." He was drowning in disappointment and confusion. "Do they still 'ave pubs?" he enquired, with an expression like a dried carp, simultaneously absurd and serious.

I nodded and smiled, welcoming the light relief. "Oh yes," I confirmed. I should have stopped there. But I didn't. "Well, of course, all the breweries have now been consolidated into global corporations. The pubs aren't like they used to be when I was a kid. It's all about brand images now."

By this time, I could tell that Ollie's mythical illusion of Earth representing some kind of Holy Grail was slowly dissolving like a tablet in a glass of water. "Do they still have music CDs?" he asked.

I shook my head.

"McDonald's?"

"Uh uh. Not any longer."

"Cricket?"

I pulled a face of regret. I was firing pellets at his dream and he was flinching.

"Pick 'n' mix?"

"No."

"Chocolate milk?"

I nodded encouragingly.

"Is it true it comes from animals? Brown cows?" He grinned widely, revealing several missing teeth. "Wait, what about football? Do they still have football?"

"Robots. You know, um, androids."

I winced as his incredulous glare fastened on me. "The referees are androids? And the linesmen?"

I shrugged. "And the players."

He said nothing, but his eyes widened like frisbees.

"But they're designed, configured and operated by humans," I added in an attempt to allay his severe concerns. I don't know why, but I felt like I was really hurting him. He asked me more questions and

I delivered a whole bunch of displeasing answers until I couldn't stand it any longer. It was like pulling wings off a butterfly or something. For no particular reason, I wondered if a butterfly with its wings removed should be called a butterwalk. Shrugging again, I made an apologetic gesture, picked up the ball and chucked it at him. "I think you'd better not ask me anything else about Earth for now. It's a lot to take in. Best to do it in small doses."

"You mean there's more bad news?"

"No, not really, just a few little things…"

"Like what?"

"Well, y'know, the usual stuff," I said, trying my best to understate the situation. "Y'know, just stuff like climate change, a bit of overpopulation here, a bit of terrorism there, land degradation, superbugs, PCBs in the food chain, the cult of unfettered economic growth and…the usual stuff."

Ollie looked at me aghast. "See, now those all sound like seriously bad things to me."

"Nah," I assured him. "It's all fine. There's still plenty of global stability. Loads of it."

"You sure? 'Cause if that's stability, I think I'd rather have some chaos."

"Nah, you just think that because you're not used to us. Hey, what are we like, eh? Ha ha!" I could tell he wasn't buying it. "Okay, maybe there *are* a few little planetary problems to sort out."

"But it's our ambition to get these Mortians to send us back there," he said, with a note of sadness and uncertainty in his voice. "Please tell me it's a better world. Isn't it a better world? We deserve a better world. Everyone 'ere talks about it *so* much. Y'know, goin' back 'ome an' all." Over the years, he and the other nefeshchayans had clearly built it up as some kind of mythological dream-world based on the stories handed down to them by their parents and grandparents. He sighed wistfully as he looked down at the shrunken basketball. "But there are obviously some 'oles in our thinkin'."

"Yeah," I said, as regretfully as I could. "I'm afraid it's full of holes. Actually, Ollie, the entire planet is probably made up of holes that people never get round to filling in." I don't know why I said that. I hadn't engaged my brain properly and, anyway, I was still fretting about Aysha and about what the hell I should do. It occurred to me to ask why, if nefeshchaya was a closed ecosystem, I had had to have the blue blood cell surgical procedure.

I suppose Ollie's explanation – that the descendants from Earth could not guarantee control of the planet if the only part of it they occupied was nefeshchaya - was plausible enough, but it placed a lot of emphasis on me getting on board with their aspirations. And why would it be so important for them to control the planet if their goal was to leave it?

After I quizzed him further about the camels and worked out he was probably talking about guanacos, we spent some time shooting baskets. Just killing time, I suppose. I don't know why we felt we had to kill time, but we did it anyway. I started to speculate if killing time might actually jeopardise eternity. And, at that point, I realised I should be doing something a bit more constructive and a little less redundant. Something a bit more sensible, at any rate…

But, hey, I couldn't be bothered.

Ollie left me alone and I carried on practising basketball with all the speed, dribbling skills and athleticism of a bowl of spilt custard. I don't think I would have scored a basket if it had been a waist-high hula-hoop. Aimlessly and ineptly lobbing and missing, I continued my slow descent into an enervating state of inner turmoil.

My main concern should have been my exile from Earth. But it wasn't. Logic and reason had given way to a harrowing sense of emotional isolation, not because I felt lonely as such – there were people around – but because I was separated from Aysha. I didn't know why Aysha had become so important to me, but she had. How exactly had that happened? I mean, have you ever walked into a friendship and forgotten what you came in for? Well, that's how I'd felt with Aysha for most of the time I'd known her. We didn't owe one another anything. We weren't an item and hadn't developed any kind of bond beyond being fairly normal friends. Well, I use the term 'normal' in the sense that Aysha used it. I had no idea what a 'normal' friend was, really. I just engaged with people in accordance with the affection and admiration I held for them. And yet here I was, discovering feelings that ran unexpectedly deep. Clearly, however, this was not a good time to start investing emotionally in her, not a good time to risk creating false perceptions. She was gone.

Well, wasn't that just typical? Maybe I'd developed an attachment to her right at the very moment when it was utterly pointless. Things like that cannot always be explained. They just happen. Who knows why or how those weird neuro-transmitters in our brains draw us to one another? Who can predict it? And who can do anything about it?

I was floundering around in a cloud of confusion, looking for signs and omens and assurances, trying to understand what they meant. I re-evaluated the relationship like I was reading a horoscope, latching onto the stuff that aligned with how I wanted things to be and dismissing the rest. All I asked was that Aysha would find life unimaginable without me! That's all. Not much to ask for, is it? Here I was, psychologically capsizing before I'd even tried to float. Sinking like an overturned boat. But, actually, not like a boat, more like a sunset, clinging sorrowfully to the western sky before yielding to the darkness. Sorry, those started out as really profound thoughts, but they were so deep that, by the time I dragged them out, they'd got all lumpy and squished.

And, as if losing Aysha wasn't devastating enough, I couldn't return to Earth either. What kind of nightmare was this? When did I get to wake up? I placed my foot firmly on the basketball and squeezed all the remaining air out of it.

PIGEON OF PEACE

Questions hummed around in my head like a swarm of rabid bees. The one that was preoccupying me at that moment was: should I take an ice bath? One of Ollie's people had suggested it after I'd complained that my muscles were aching like crazy. The introduction of blue blood cells into my circulation had caused a build-up of lactic acid and an ice bath can help to flush away the lactate and reduce tissue breakdown.

Okay, so there were certainly more important questions for me to address, but, well, I have a well-known and much-criticised propensity for homing in on the minutiae of life. When I was ten years old, I came home from school to find our family kitchen destroyed owing to a chip fryer being left unattended. As my parents looked aghast at the blackened ceiling and walls, I didn't endear myself to them by pestering them with my genuine and heart-felt concern for the chips.

Anyway, no ice bath. I settled for an iced coffee.

"You can do a job for us," said someone I assumed to be John. This assumption was based purely on my observation that he yelled a lot at the others and was therefore clearly some kind of authority figure. "You can act as a lai-uson, er, lease-alien, er …"

"Liaison?" I suggested.

"Go-between," said John, "between us and the Mortians. We need to get 'em to co-operate."

It all sounded a bit daunting. "I don't suppose I could just teach them a useful craft like pottery or macramé or a hobby like fishkeeping?" I asked.

John had the appearance of someone who would gladly make fools suffer, someone who would fight fire with fire and not, you know, water. A tall, big-boned man with a prominent forehead and jaw, long, wiry hair and a grey and white beard, he looked like the sort of man who didn't smile very often. I wondered if he had problems with teeth crowding or bad gums and I wondered if he should force the odd smile for the sake of his mental health. If you trick your body with a forced smile, would you trigger the same release of endorphins as you would if it were a genuine impulse?

We were sitting in a mock-up Irish bar, eating burgers. Obviously, it wasn't the same mock-up Irish bar as the one where the Mortians were locked up. It was another one. I don't know how they could justify having more than one of them. It was certainly confusing. Gradually, I managed to relax a little. One of the walls featured a rugby-themed mural. I took in my surroundings and observed the interactions around me. The nefeshchayans were a motley bunch of oddities, armed with assorted weapons seized during the insurrection. There were a few bad apples – not just the metaphorical ones, although that was probably the case, but actual real apples with discoloured spots and wrinkled skin placed in bowls on the dark wood tables. The burger actually tasted quite good. Mid-bite, however, I stopped and wondered what meat I was eating. The only non-human life forms I'd spotted on the planet so far were blanids and spherical-shaped orbis birds that rolled themselves off the tops of dwelling pods. I really prayed that I wasn't chewing a blanid. "What do you actually want the Mortians to *do*?" I asked.

"We want 'em to send us 'ome," said John, tapping his fingers on the arm of his chair, beating out a nervous rhythm.

I should have asked someone what I was eating, but I didn't. "Why *wouldn't* they send you home?" I asked, turning to Ollie, who shot me a fleeting glance and turned away, a shadow of misgiving clouding his face. "They'd be glad to see the back of you, wouldn't they?"

John's brow puckered in consternation. "No," he

said. "I dunno why, but for some reason, they reckon they need us 'ere. Also, they probably think we've got an axe to grind."

"Well, you *have* imprisoned them on their own planet," I pointed out. "How do you intend to resolve that? What are you going to do with them?"

John smirked. "Er, rehabilitate 'em? Turn 'em into productive members of society?" The other nefeshchayans laughed. "I dunno. That's why we're gonna need *you*. It's all gotta be done peaceful-like. You gotta explain that we're not doin' this 'cause we're thirstin' for revenge or anythin'. We didn't want to take over their planet, except temporary-like - just so we could persuade 'em to send us back to Earth. And we 'ave no intention of comin' back 'ere later with a formidable task force to overpower 'em again and rule the planet. Nothin' like that."

"Um, you do realise we haven't got anywhere close to mastering wormhole technology back on Earth?" I pointed out, frowning at the absurdity of the idea. "The idea that we could send a task force here is just laughable. The Mortians must *know* that. And if they didn't know it before, they certainly know it now, because yukawa3 will have told them. He's, y'know, well aware of our limitations in that respect." They were all staring at me as if I'd just beamed down from, well, Earth. "And, anyway," I shrugged, "*no one* can get to this planet at the moment. No one at all. That's right isn't it, Ollie?"

Ollie nodded. "Yeah," he said. "It's one-way traffic only. I zapped the incoming transport controls. You can get incoming *voice* transmissions, but that's all."

"What? Why?" snarled John, throwing his arms wide in a gesture of exasperation.

Adopting a slightly defensive tone, Ollie argued that there might have been other Mortians awaiting transport back to Melinda, so he had used his initiative and forestalled the possibility of a Mortian rescue mission.

"But they're all 'ere! We captured twenty-nine of 'em and the one that was brought back from Earth made it thirty - the entire population."

"Well, 'ow was I supposed to know that?" said Ollie truculently. "Okay, okay, I made a mistake. I'm not perfect."

"Not even close."

"I know I need to improve in one or two areas."

"Three or four," said John and then added, "'undred."

"I've got what it takes, don' you worry," Ollie insisted. "I'll show you. If we can't get back to Earth, this planet is gonna need a Secretary of Defence and…"

John was having none of it. "Really? Are you kiddin' me? Secretary of Defence? You can't even spell it! What will you do? Release your inner Churchill? May I remind you your nickname round 'ere is 'Mad Dog'!"

"Well, you know what? Mark my words - Defence Secretary. Nothin's gonna stop me."

"Until you get distracted by somethin' else," scoffed John. "Somethin' shiny." The others laughed.

Ollie cast a look of earnest appeal at the assembled company. "These people," he said. "These people know they can trust me to do the right thing."

John's riposte was scathing. "Sure. After you've tried everythin' else."

I don't know why I felt compelled to spring to Ollie's defence, but I did so anyway. "Give him a break," I said. "Even if I can persuade them to do it, you're not going to just *trust* the Mortians to send you back to Earth, are you? You're going to need someone to monitor what they're doing. Ollie here obviously knows a bit about the wormhole controls."

"Enough to zap 'em to bits!" sneered John, sotto voce.

"Well, yeah," I countered, "but the point is he knew *which* bits to zap."

His hands in his trouser pockets, thumbs protruding, John turned to Ollie. "'Well, 'ow *did* you know?" he enquired, with a slight raising of his eyebrows.

"That's for me to know and you to worry about," said Ollie, sounding more than a little morose. "Anyway, I should 'ave some kind of position. You're the 'igh commander and Nigel is bar manager and Jess is 'ead of creative services. Everybody else 'as got some kind of title. So what am I?"

"Well," said John, "you're Ollie."

"Yeah, great title. What's my *role*? What am I responsible for?"

"That's it," said John. "That's the problem. You're irresponsible!"

By now, I simply had to ask. "What *am* I eating?"

"Orbis bird," said a woman with dark hair, a skull

tattooed on her left cheek.

"Have you got anything for vegetarians?" I asked, recalling that the orbis birds I'd seen were fat and scaly. Worse than that, they were yellow with angry-looking red patches and, well, they looked thoroughly unappetising. "Moral reasons," I added superfluously.

"Dunno," the woman replied, giving me a very quizzical look. "Hey, Lizzie! Have we got anything for vegetarians?"

"Yeah," came the reply. "Hunger!" The two women shrieked with laughter.

As the others began to lose interest and dispersed to various corners of the bar, I asked Ollie discreetly, "So, go on, tell me! How *did* you know which controls to zap?"

"The doodles," he said, coughing violently. "The weird markings on the panel."

"The hieroglyphic things? What about them?"

A fit of spluttering, coughing and spitting delayed his reply. "They match the entry and exit markings the Mortians put on the perimeter gates. They 'ave a one-way system 'cos they're always collidin'. Have you seen 'em drivin' those magnetic propulsion cruiser things? 'Opeless!"

I suppose I could say his recognition of the hieroglyphics demonstrated impressive observation skills, but then I figured out the reason for his coughing - he'd mistaken the chilli sauce bottle for ketchup.

The evening wore on and got darker, as evenings are wont to do. I figured that acting as a mediator in this dispute was kind of consistent with my wider remit as Earth's ambassador, so I consented to John's proposal. "Will I have to wear a suit?" I asked. "I didn't bring one."

Evidently John took this as a kind of rhetorical question and proceeded to drum into my head a whole bunch of questions for the Mortians, such as: 'how can safe arrival on Earth be assured and verified?', 'how many Mortians are skilled at operating the gateway technology?', 'how many people can be transported at one time?', 'can you get wormhole traffic jams?' and 'do any of these bars have pork scratchings?'. Okay, the last of those didn't come from John – they just sprung into my head for some reason. After I'd clarified exactly what I was expected to do in terms of liaising with the Mortians, I went outside to witness the second of the two sunsets blazing behind a veil of curling black clouds.

As I gazed towards the dramatic horizon, my

thoughts returned to Aysha and a deep melancholy enveloped my soul. Recollecting a few random examples of her warmth towards me, I wondered what trail of thoughts had gone through her head when she had decided to leave. Sure, she had changing moods and could be a little confusing and unpredictable, but no one would have described her as erratic or unstable, prone to being blown off course by winds of emotion. I just didn't think there was anything in her makeup that might seriously cloud her judgment in such a way. So, what had happened? What irresistible wave of impulse had swept her to such a course of action?

Off in the distance, I spotted a few small creatures – possibly blanids – emerging and nipping at something on the ground, lean low bodies creeping around like tiny ninjas, then scattering like skittish fish. Suddenly, the stillness was rent by the call of an orbis bird, eerie and piercing, sending a sudden streak of chills up and down my spine. A few minutes later, I heard it again, this time away in the distance. One of the planet's three moons emerged from the top of the anguished-looking invercresco trees. I wondered if Aysha was gazing at the night sky through the curtains of her bedroom window back on Earth. And I wondered what she was thinking.

The next thing I knew, I received a sharp blow to

the back of my head. Grasping the wound, I whirled around to see a bird beating its wings just a few feet away from me. Before I had time to figure out what was happening, it swooped again. I ducked and started to run back towards the door, my hands flapping wildly above my head as the bird attacked, repeatedly pecking at my hair.

On reaching the safety of the bar, I slumped into a chair and the tattooed woman tended to my wounds.

"Nesting material," she explained. "Should've warned you. They'll go for anything - hair, bits of cloth, wool, tissue. An' they don't wait for no invitation!"

"I think I'll have that burger now!" I said, feeling battered, aggrieved and, well, vengeful.

"The bird what attacked you weren't no orbis bird," the woman pointed out. "Orbis birds don't 'ave a beak."

"So what *was* it then?"

Having completed her repairs, the woman patted me reassuringly on the shoulder and said, "It was a pigeon."

"A pigeon?" I echoed, astounded. "As in, like, a New York kind of pigeon? A London pigeon? Trafalgar Square? Feed the birds, tuppence a bag?"

The woman nodded. "Yeah," she said. "The Mortians abducted some of them from Earth years and years ago, thinking they were doves."

"Why did they want doves?"

"Their research told 'em doves was thought of as symbols of peace, so they thought… well, I guess they thought if they introduced 'em into nefeshchaya, it would calm us down or somefin'."

"Good grief." I muttered and then added a misquotation for no good reason whatsoever: "The pigeon, on silver pinions, winged her peaceful way."

"Yeah," she went on. "So we've been stuck with 'em ever since."

"Pigeons don't behave like this on Earth," I said. "Okay, they can be a bit of a pain. Some people consider them to be airborne vermin, but at least the ones on Earth don't go around pecking people and stealing their hair!"

"I've never been to Earth, so I wouldn't know *how* they're s'posed to behave, would I?"

No," I shrugged. "And, to be fair, nor would that pigeon."

John was rubbing his chin. "Ollie!" he called. "I've

got it! I've found a role for you. You are now officially our pigeon exterminator!"

Ollie looked singularly unimpressed. "Pigeon exterminator?" he complained. "That sounds like a really naff job."

"It's an order!" said John emphatically.

"Fine," said Ollie with all the enthusiasm of someone about to have a colonoscopy.

"Don't look so concerned," said John. "It's an important job and it pays well."

Ollie looked perplexed and protested, "But I thought we were all paid the same. Aren't we? Wait, are you paid more than the rest of us?"

"Just a little more, maybe."

"'Ow much more?"

John shrugged. "A lot more."

THE LIMITS OF THE DIPLOMATIC ARENA

When John unlocked the door to the bar where the Mortians were being held, I stepped in apprehensively. The high-vaulted ceiling and a spectacular crank-open, stained-glass skylight immediately caught my eye. Spirals of dust danced lazily past a golf mural on the wall. The Mortians were assembled around a cluster of dark wood tables near a stone fireplace. No one noticed me; they were all staring fixedly at a corpulent figure draped in a long garland of glistening seaweed, sporting an eye patch and a misshapen, asymmetric, coin-encrusted helmet. Later, I was informed that this was, in fact, a *sherg*-encrusted helmet. I didn't know what a sherg was – it looked vaguely like a twentieth century twelve-sided threepenny bit. He was twirling an umbrella. Even though yukawa3 (and casimir2) had described the planetary leader to me on several occasions, it was still a considerable shock to behold him sagging like a punctured zeppelin in that armchair. So this was the legendary polkingbeal67 I'd heard so much about. If there's such a word as underawed, then I was underawed. I had kind of expected my first encounter with him to be like a sighting of the last unicorn. But it wasn't. He was about as impressive as a juggler on the radio. Suffice to say, the impression he made on me was about as strong as a moth bite.

Before I indulge myself too much in the luxury of criticising the leader of an alien planet, I guess I should acknowledge the staggeringly volatile and idiosyncratic style of some of the heads of state we have witnessed in recent times back on Earth – the likes of Kim Jong-un, Donald Trump, Mark Cuban, Zhang Wei, Alexei Navalny and Alejandro Garcia. Our culture of celebrity politics has led to some bizarre and dangerous consequences. So, someone from Earth, like myself, is hardly in a position to cast the first stone.

One thing was decidedly strange about polkingbeal67 though. According to my grandmother's account of events, he had lost an eye way back in Mortian history at the battle of Hat Signs. But he and smolin9 had exchanged bodies, so, as far as I was aware, there was subsequently no need for him to be wearing an eye patch. Also, smolin9 had not been even remotely corpulent. Questions were popping up and disappearing in my head like ducks in a fairground gallery.

"…and what I say is this," he was telling the assembled group. "We must act fast. It's just a matter of time before we're too late. Two days from now, tomorrow will be yesterday."

I suddenly remembered my grandmother's portrayal of polkingbeal67's predecessor as a 'smelly nincompoop who talked in Chinese fortune cookies'. Apparently, polkingbeal67 was carrying on the former leader's legacy.

On noticing me, he made as if to get up, but evidently found it to be too much effort. A furious thrashing of limbs ensued, punctuated by gasps of tortured breathing. When his mouth started opening and closing like a dying fish, I contemplated the possibility that this was some kind of alien social etiquette. But it went on for so long. Wait, was I witnessing a peculiar display of Mortian performance art? Eventually, without saying a word, he gestured feebly with his umbrella until the other Mortians surrounded me and motioned me towards their leader's chair. For a few moments, no one moved or said a word. It was as if we were all transfixed in time. Then polkingbeal67 tapped the point of his umbrella on the floor.

Casimir2's voice fractured the silence. "You... you heard our revered leader!" he squawked. "Seize him!" I hadn't actually heard polkingbeal67 utter a single word, and some of the other Mortians looked at one another in bewilderment. None of them laid a hand on me. Bizarrely, I noticed a penguin, head enveloped in a yellow sou'wester, lurking in a corner, desperately trying to avoid being noticed – not easy, I guess, for a penguin in a yellow sou'wester.

"I don't need to be seized," I said, as engagingly as I could. "I'm an ambassador from Earth. I just want to talk to you."

Polkingbeal67 leaned forward and stared at me suspiciously with his 'good' eye, presumably to see if I looked dangerous. Turning to casimir2, he mumbled something I didn't quite catch.

Casimir2 gave a derisory sniff. "Seize him!" he screeched.

"Do I have the right to remain silent?" I asked, for no particular reason.

One of the Mortians reached out and tentatively plucked at my sleeve and this seemed to satisfy casimir2. Polkingbeal67 sat back with an air of bemused contentment. "You are descended from your grandmother, Melinda," he informed me, as if I didn't already know. "So, we mean you no harm whatsoever. You have inherited a reputation I trust you can live up to. If reputation has value, you are indeed a wealthy man." He finished with a conciliatory wink. At least, I *think* it was a wink –

when someone's wearing an eye patch, it's not easy to tell. Honestly, I couldn't tell whether or not this was a sincere attempt on his part to acknowledge a connection with me, but I smiled as pleasantly as I could and offered my hand, only for polkingbeal67 to place his umbrella in it. I accepted it gingerly, wondering what on earth I was supposed to do with it. Around me, the Mortians gave little nods of encouragement, so I pushed the slider up and opened the canopy.

Casimir2 uttered an unearthly howl, polkingbeal67 clamped his hands on the armrests of the chair and the other Mortians started milling around in disarray. I hastily collapsed the umbrella and handed it back to polkingbeal67, bowing like a courtier. I have no idea why I did the bowing thing. Clearly struggling to strike a balance between stilted diplomacy and sheer antagonism, casimir2 snarled at me with a gravelly squawk and said, "You must respect our leader! My bona fide advice to you is to… is to listen. Pay attention to what he's going to say to you!"

After some systematic fidgeting with the umbrella, polkingbeal67 shifted his eye between me and casimir2. Finally, he intoned solemnly, "What I'm about to say must never be repeated to anyone. To forget one's ancestors is to be a river without a source, a tree without roots. Face your future without fear. Focus on your blessings, not your misfortunes."

"Absolutely," I said. "Listen, I'm sure we're going to get along just fine. Y'know, polkingbeal67 is a little bit of a mouthful. Is it okay if I call you PB?"

With his one eye, he eyed me with that cold, contemptuous look a predator has when eyeing its prey. "No," he said.

"PB67?"

"No."

Obviously, I was impressed that my grandmother was held in such high esteem by the planetary leader, but it was becoming clear that this liaison role of mine was going to present some problems.

Anyway, polkingbeal67 and I were engaged for some time in a profound discussion of matters I can only describe as completely unintelligible. I spent most of the time praying for someone or something to interrupt us, but nothing happened. His moods swung from lucid and amenable one moment to distracted and preoccupied the next. And the switches occurred randomly and at breakneck speed. It was a bizarre experience, only marginally more enjoyable than a protracted visit to the dentist.

"You're completely safe here," he told me. "We're

used to you earthlings now. We have no wish to dissect you for scientific research."

"I appreciate that," I said. Okay, I probably should have come up with something better.

"Just explain one thing for me."

"Sure."

"Are you aware that your grandmother had my heart?"

"Yes."

"Well, why was she cremated?"

"Um, she was dead," I replied. I should probably have taken a moment or two longer and thought about it first, but there it is.

His face went slack and he turned away from me. "Would you mind terribly if I asked you to leave?" he said after a short pause.

"I'm sorry, but that's just what we do on Earth when people die."

"I demand an explanation!" he bellowed.

"I just gave you one."

The silence that ensued was deafening. Eventually,

I decided to cut to the chase: "Are you willing to send them home to Earth?"

"Who?"

"These people. The people you've kept imprisoned here."

"I'm *their* prisoner," said polkingbeal67, his hackles rising. "They must release *us* first. I must be allowed to return to the palace of obsidian fingers."

"Well, yeah," I mumbled. "It's just a question of sorting out the logistics - they release you, and you arrange for them to return to Earth. Everyone's happy. Yes? No?"

"You can make your own happiness. All things are difficult before they are easy," said polkingbeal67, sounding as cryptic as ever. Many of his fortune cookie quotes were completely random, so I never really knew how much attention to pay to them, but, evidently, he wanted to make something out of this situation. Kudos from the intergalactic community? I couldn't work it out, but it was apparent that he had an agenda of his own, one that he didn't want to share with me at that moment.

My patience was starting to run about as thin as the seaweed that enswathed his massive frame. "Listen," I said, irritation making my voice scratchy. "I'm sorry, but we're obviously having trouble communicating."

"I don't know what you're talking about."

"Yeah, that's kinda what I mean," I suggested. "Let me speak to yukawa3?"

"You want to improve our communication by talking to someone else?"

"No, but… yes! Yeah, it's not you, it's just… it's me. It's my fault. Let me talk to yukawa3."

"That's a no-can-do," said polkingbeal67. "I think we should give it another try. Maybe we should share feelings, open up to one another. After all, if we are to work together, we must become better acquainted."

Was that last bit a fortune cookie thing? I had no idea. All I knew was that I couldn't cope with polkingbeal67 any longer.

"Deep down inside, I'm just this fat guy who wants to be loved at all costs," he revealed with a sudden, bizarre effusion of candour, twirling the umbrella between his long fingers and affecting a look of bovine openness. "What about you?"

Thrown off balance, I found myself drawn into this utterly weird and otherworldly conversation. "Um,

I've got a tattoo?" I ventured uncertainly.

Polkingbeal67 leaned forward and murmured into my ear conspiratorially, "I have to command these people, so I don't wish to say this aloud, but I want you to know… that I understand." He waited for a second or two, presumably for some encouragement from me and then continued, "If I didn't have to maintain the dignity of my office as a planetary leader, I'd take you in my arms and hold you like a little bunny wabbit."

"Wh-what!" I exclaimed in disbelief. "This isn't right. I don't understand. What's going on?" I looked around to see if any of the Mortians had spotted this alarming lapse. Thankfully, there was no giggling, nudging or winking. In fact, no one was paying any attention to us at all.

"You will strike it very, very rich one day," promised polkingbeal67.

"Yeah, well," I said, "I want to be rich in dignity. I'm a grown man and I really don't want to be referred to as a…" I couldn't bring myself to say it.

"A bunny wabbit?"

"Yes. That."

"Would you like a carrot?" polkingbeal67 asked, without a trace of flippancy. Noticing the look of astonishment on my face, he added, "They grow them here using the most responsible environmentally-friendly farming methods."

"No," I insisted as forcefully as I could. "I don't want a carrot! I want… I want to negotiate your release and the safe transmission of your captors back to Earth."

"They won't like it there."

"You're probably right," I acknowledged. "But can we please talk about it?"

"Okay, certainly," said polkingbeal67. Was he about to have an episode of something approaching lucidity? "Sorry about the wabbit thing."

"Well," I said, dubiously, not knowing what was coming next. "Okay then. Right. I'm willing to overlook it."

"It's just that I thought you earthlings thought wabbits were engaging and agreeable."

"Rabbits," I corrected him. "Not wabbits."

"And do you people find them engaging and agreeable?"

"Well, yes," I said hesitantly. "But bear in mind we eat them."

"You eat bunny wabbits?"

"Rabbits. Yes."

"Even though you find them engaging and agreeable?"

"Yes, but we also keep them as pets and sing songs about them." For reasons that now elude me, I started humming a few bars of 'Bright Eyes'.

"...and then you eat them?" Polkingbeal67's 'good' eye was wide with amazement.

"You people eat orbis birds," I countered indignantly.

"That's true," said polkingbeal67, examining the point of his umbrella reflectively. "But we don't sing songs about them. Which is a pity in a way. I've always wanted to play the accordion."

Not for the last time, I found myself careering off on one of polkingbeal67's tangents. "Well, why don't you? What's stopping you? Music is wonderful. Music is like taking a blank silence and painting sounds on it to create an emotional soundscape. Listen, you're the product of an advanced civilisation, aren't you? The ability to create music should be child's play to you."

Polkingbeal67 pursed his lips. "I don't have an

accordion," he said. "Anyway, you're preaching to the converted. My interplanetary profile lists my interests as yoga, long walks and classical music."

How had I allowed myself to get so side-tracked and distracted? I had to refocus and get back on track. "Listen, can I tell them you'll send them back to Earth?"

"It's not as easy as that."

"Why not?"

"We need them here."

I think my expression was probably a mixture of bewilderment and some other, better word meaning, well, bewilderment. "You *need* them here?"

"We Mortians are not the complete package," he clarified, glancing cautiously around the room. "You probably think we're outstanding specimens of humanoid perfection?"

"Well, I…"

"Not a single molecule of DNA out of place?"

"Um…"

"Thing is, we're deficient in certain key hormones." Motioning me closer, he added in a whisper, "Sometimes it brings us out in the most terrible rash."

So, given the way he kept scratching, twitching and glancing nervously over towards the other Mortians, I figured he was afflicted to a greater degree than his peers.

"But you're the leader," I protested. "I'm sure they'd be supportive if you just explained it to them."

"I feel ignored and forgotten," he confided. "My position here is tenuous, very tenuous. Perilous, actually."

Assuming this was a good place to nod, I nodded.

Lowering his voice, he went on in precise, measured syllables, fingering the battered helmet perched a little cheekily on his head. "This is no way to treat a war hero, someone who fought for his planet, someone who should be remembered. You see this helmet? This helmet saw action at Tharsis Crater on Ynonmaq Decimus. This helmet dodged ionizer blasts during the liberation of chilloks in the Fourth Intergalactic War and then mysteriously disappeared."

"Why was it a mystery?"

"Because I didn't tell anyone."

"Did it actually disappear?"

"Of course not," said polkingbeal67, looking irritated.

I wanted the two of us to get off to a good start, so I left it there.

"This helmet has seen some famous action," he said. "Those days were like, you know…"

"Well, it certainly looks like it's been in a few very bad places," I concurred.

Removing the helmet and contemplating it with an air of dignity and pride, he went on, "It got severely dented during the charge against General Vog in the famous defeat of the Trox army at Ybesan." He offered it for my inspection.

I felt strangely drawn to this mesmerising character. "I tore a pair of trainers in a game of touch rugby once," I disclosed. "It was tough. They were a birthday present."

Leaning forward, he clapped a hand on my shoulder, his eye red and misty. "We are two of a kind. We are kindred spirits. We have both endured journeys of untold danger and hardship…"

"Yes, I guess so," I said. "But it was just touch rugby."

"Agony, fear and despair," he continued, squeezing my shoulder.

"Hmm. Are you kiddin' me? Absolutely." I tried to think of something pertinent to say, but nothing came. And then it did. "I'm allergic to peanuts."

Polkingbeal67 nodded sympathetically. I'm fairly sure he didn't know what I was talking about.

Out of the corner of my eye, I became aware that the other Mortians were huddled around casimir2, engaged in hushed conversation.

"They've turned against me," polkingbeal67 lamented. "When a tree falls, the monkeys scatter. I don't know what to do. I've lost myself, lost my sense of identity. I spend sleepless nights worrying about it. And then there's the rash." He pointed it out – a few green-grey patches on his arms. Slumping back in the chair, he stared desolately from his pudgy eye and sighed like a tormented spirit sinking into the dark abyss of existential crisis.

It kind of struck a chord with me. Tears of displaced commiseration and pity brimmed in my eyes. Inexplicably overcome with mawkish feelings of empathy, I suddenly announced, "I've been a vegetarian for years." At that moment, it just seemed an appropriately touchy-feely thing to say. I can only explain the onset of this weirdness in terms of my realisation that I was flummoxed by everything, including my role as mediator.

Glancing over at casimir2 and back again to polkingbeal67, I started to wonder if I was talking to the right person. Polkingbeal67 did not appear to hold sway over the rest of the Mortians. Could he be considered a leader when, apparently, no one was following? Or was something else going on here, something I didn't yet understand? "Why don't you just seize control?" I said. "Take some initiative."

"You're right." He lowered his head and nodded. "I think I need a cigarette."

Well, that threw me, I must admit. "A cigarette?" I echoed. "You smoke cigarettes here?"

"From your planet, yes. We acquired them for research purposes. Enough food and a pipe full of tobacco makes you equal to the immortals. But you should do something about the pictures."

"The pictures?"

"Yes, the pictures on the side of the pack. They're gruesome. Enough to put you off smoking for life."

The reference to such a trite but archetypal facet of earthling life bewildered me for a moment. And, anyway, there was no doubt about it - I was in the process of establishing a new agenda of my own. How did I really feel about facilitating the departure of the nefeshchayans? If my future lay here on planet Melinda (and apparently, having had my heart surgically reconfigured, it did), could I contemplate such a future without the fellowship of my own kind? I couldn't deny that their presence offered a comforting measure of security against the hazards and uncertainties of my new environment.

I dreaded the debriefing session with John, so I hung around with polkingbeal67 for way longer than I needed to. At one point, I confided some of my misgivings to him.

Fixing me with a look I couldn't quite get a handle on, he leaned closer and said, "You want to help me trick the nefeshchayan insurgents?"

"No," I said. "I don't think so. Do I? No, I'm not sure."

"You want to trick *me*?" he suggested, nodding furiously in encouragement.

"Yes," I said emphatically.

"I appreciate your honesty." He spoke in a tone void of emotion.

Totally confused, I promptly changed my mind.

"No, no, not really," I assured him. "I'm not used to being in this kind of situation, and I just don't know what to do. I want to do the right thing. I just can't make up my mind what that is."

Polkingbeal67 twiddled his umbrella. "Don't worry about procrastinating," he said, settling back in his chair, clearly relishing the opportunity to entertain a captive audience. "Let me tell you the story of swither15 of the mythical Land of Loit. He was the seventh son of a seventh son." Pausing to check if I was paying attention, he added, "I don't want to bore you."

"Hmm, too late," I thought, mischievously.

He continued: "Swither15 never went out fishing with his brothers, but spent his days rowing around in his own boat, making up wild stories about sea monsters. One day, a real fire-breathing sea dragon emerged from the waves and threatened to set fire to one of the boats. Legend has it that the dragon couldn't decide which boat to set ablaze and commanded swither15 to choose one of them. Unable to make up his mind, swither15 pondered and pondered until the dragon got bored and fell asleep and they all escaped. To this day, the word 'switherer' is used in colloquial Mortian to denote a person who procrastinates in the face of the enemy. There is a Mortian proverb - 'better to be a switherer for a few minutes than dead for the rest of your life'". Following this with a sigh that seemed to come from the very depths of his being, he added, "But you've only got two hours."

"What?" I asked in confusion. "Two hours to do what?"

"Get me out of here!" he yelled at the top of his lungs, smashing his fist down in rage and frustration. Pieces of the helmet flew like shrapnel across the table. Recovering his composure as quickly as he had lost it, he added, "I want you to know that my door is always open. Oh, um, except when it's locked by the nefeshchayans. Um, like it is now."

Remember I mentioned seeing a penguin with a sou'wester? Okay, well, I just didn't want that to get lost in all of this.

LIFTED

Having persuaded John that I needed a bit of time and space to formulate a plan of action, I received a quick lesson from casimir2 (under Ollie's supervision) in how to drive a Mortian land cruiser. As the double sunrise of my third day on Melinda painted itself across the horizon, I sped away from the nefeshchaya compound, relishing the feeling that I had escaped from everyone on the planet, albeit just for a few hours.

Once I'd been escorted through the perimeter gates of the enclosure, I was soon hurtling past the Mortian habitation pods across the shelterless rocky terrain until I reached the top of a rise where the scrub thinned out a little. Sitting on the bonnet of the cruiser, I surveyed the alien landscape that lay before me. This was a lowland region formed where tectonic plates had evidently moved apart. On the northern horizon, a steep scarp was cut by deep erosional valleys. The sunlight glinted off a couple of large liquid methane lakes, and a soft breeze whipped some dust and sand around the low-lying scrub thickets.

Temporarily relieved of the more immediate and

pressing challenges besetting me, my mind fluttered like a moth helplessly and fatally drawn to a campfire. Finally, fascinated by the light, it settled on thoughts of Aysha.

As far as I was concerned, Aysha and I had been developing the most awesome friendship and I figured it would take quite some time for me to process the loss properly. Trying my very best not to feel bitter or angry, I revisited everything that had happened. Surely, she might have handled it better? Surely, she could have waited to say a proper goodbye face-to-face? In any case, how could she be so sure I wouldn't have returned to Earth with her? Hell, let's face it, I almost certainly *would* have returned with her if I'd failed to persuade her to stay a while! But I really didn't want to get consumed with a pile of negative stuff right now. I was already struggling to control the sadness that gripped my heart and held it fast.

I became aware of a tiny scuttling shape out of the corner of my eye. Some kind of insect. Whatever it was, it quickly disappeared behind a rock. Then I noticed a kind of spider web trail between the rock and a piece of scrub about four feet away. It wasn't like a spider's web on Earth. It was stickier, more fibrous. Bits of it were almost jelly-like, trembling in the breeze.

I'd felt a strong connection with Aysha right from when we first got to know each other, and I'd just wanted us to be the best buddies of all time. I'd set out to be the kind of friend I would have loved to have had. I guess every friendship is like a voyage of discovery, but perhaps, without realising it, I'd been doing nearly all the driving. And perhaps we hadn't been heading anywhere she wanted to go.

Obviously, I had forgotten many of the things my grandmother had said to me when I was growing up, but I *do* remember her saying this: if you find someone who makes you smile, someone who checks up on you regularly to see if you're okay, someone who has your back - you shouldn't let them go. You should keep them close and avoid taking them for granted. She told me people like that are hard to find. When Aysha and I became friends, I tried, tried really hard, to be one of those people my grandmother had referred to.

Anyway, you probably don't want to hear all this. Besides, it was all water under the bridge now and maybe Aysha already had other 'hard to find' people in her life. Honestly, I hoped that was the case. As for me, outside of my family, I didn't have anyone like that. I guess I'd been hoping Aysha might have been one of them - one of those special 'hard to find' people.

Was something else going on? Had my limbic system been messing with me? No, I told myself, that's so ridiculous. Silver whispers and nightingales? Give me strength! I hadn't been looking for the clouds to part or the starlight to dance on the waves or anything like that. Totally ridiculous. But, you know what? Perhaps that was it. Perhaps something else *was* going on. I tried to dismiss the thought, but it's pointless trying to tell a heart how to feel. It won't listen. Hearts may or may not have wings; they certainly don't have ears. As the twin suns climbed higher in the clear blue sky, the ache in my heart forced a lump to my throat and tears welled up.

I gazed again at the web trail and my mind started drifting. Spiders. Webs. Dreamcatchers. According to Native American lore, the spider was considered to be a spirit of creativity. The original dreamcatchers, woven in the nineteenth century by tribal artisans, were symbolic webs, intended to trap bad dreams and nightmares, allowing only good dreams through.

Exhausted and plagued by an oppressive sense of hopelessness and helplessness, I slid onto the warm rock below the web and, as the suns beat down, I closed my eyes and immersed myself in a flood of memories in an effort to lift my spirits.

. . .

When I awoke, the web had gone. So had the suns. Turbulent whirls of sand raged across the landscape, whipped and buffeted by a vicious wind. Flurries of grainy particles lashed my face and whistled in my ears. Jumping to my feet, I ran to the cruiser but it wouldn't start. These vehicles weren't like anything on Earth – they had no wheels, for one thing, and they used magnetic propulsion, for another. Obviously, something was clogged, so I hunkered down in the driver's seat to wait out the storm.

An hour or so passed. The cyclone receded, and the cruiser was now buried in a dune of sand that reached halfway up the gull-wing doors, which refused to open. A wave of panic slowly spread over me. They say there's nothing to fear except fear itself, but, I tell you what, being buried alive bothers me a bit. I'm also not too keen on seeing shark fins when I'm swimming, or zombies (whether I'm swimming or not), or clowns, or brain-eating parasites.

You would think there must have been all manner of sophisticated communication devices on this planet, so why the devil hadn't they given me one? Why wasn't there one built into the cruiser? Perhaps there was. But, despite twiddling, turning, tapping and pressing everything on the control panel, I couldn't get anything to spring into life except a flickering interior light. Okay, that's not entirely true. At one point, I touched something that appeared to trigger a vexed and rather hostile voice, like a fox squealing through a vocoder. I had no idea what it was.

Like a wildebeest in the clutches of a lion, I was almost resigned to my fate when the cruiser started shaking like a bowl of jelly in an earthquake. Creaking. The sound of suction. A rocking sensation. And then I figured it out – the cruiser was being pulled out of the sand by means of some kind of tractor beam. For a while, the creaking got so bad, I started to suspect serious structural damage to the hull, but then the sand sighed and relinquished its grip. For some reason, I activated the gull-wing doors and they sprang open. So there I was, inside a cruiser that was hovering above the ground like a great robotic falcon searching for its prey.

. . .

"There you are!" said casimir2 more than an hour later when he finally managed to switch off the tractor beam. His face was contorted into a sickly attempt at an ingratiating smile. "Did you have trouble parking? Anyway, it does my heart good to see you… to see you safe and sound. I bet you're glad you've got your feet back on terra firma."

"What the hell?" I exclaimed, trying to extricate myself from the most awkward and smelly hug of all time. I was so creeped out. And he used both arms. Gross.

"I'm just trying to be warm and nurturing," said casimir2. "Are you okay? That's a great sweater, by the way... a great sweater."

"It's not a sweater. It's a tunic, and I've been wearing it the whole time I've been here. What the hell?"

"Do you have one in leopard print?"

"No!"

"Can I try it on?" asked casimir2, fingering it with his carbuncled fingers. "Please!"

"No!" I asserted. "Don't you have weather forecasts on this infernal planet? Why did you leave me without any means of communication?"

Casimir2 whirled his arms around for no obvious reason. "We knew what was brewing and we were monitoring you all the time... all the time," he said, obviously vexed by my exasperated questions. He gestured meaningfully towards his microwocky.

When I duly enquired about this mysterious piece of Mortian technology, he happily went off on a tangent, launching into a complete description of all its features - microplasma and nanomanufacturing technology, shape-shifting capability, a profusion of holographic telepresence feeds and all the rest of it. To be honest, the only word I understood was 'feed'. I hadn't had any breakfast. Anyway, it was allegedly "the most genius piece of technology ever seen."

"Look," he said. "This is currently showing on our main news channel." A sub-screen displayed magnified 3D high definition video images of the Mortian landscape.

"Wow!" I muttered sarcastically. "Yeah, that's impressive. It's almost like being there."

"Well, yes... yes, we *are* there," said casimir2, as his own face loomed into view on the sub-screen.

"Well, in that case, it's not quite so impressive, is it?" I remarked, ramping up the sarcasm. "Listen, if you were monitoring what was going on, why the hell... What, for God's sake, took you so long?" That wasn't the question I should have asked. The question I should have asked was: "Why did you let me take the cruiser out if you knew a storm was coming?"

Casimir2 gestured theatrically at Ollie who was pointing a long, double-barrelled laser weapon at him. "These people wouldn't let us rescue you."

"That's not true," contradicted Ollie. "It was *your* fault. You insisted on comin' out 'ere alone, knowin' full well we wouldn't let you…"

"But you'll die out here!" casimir2 pointed out.

"That's true, isn't it, Ollie?" I said. "And I have to say you're looking decidedly peaky, mate."

Ollie, who was shaking and had dark half-moons under his eyes, pursed his lips and looked at casimir2 with a glazed expression for a few seconds. "Yeah," he said. "I'm not feelin' too good. We gotta get back."

"I'm not… I'm not going back!" announced casimir2 with conviction.

I guess it was at this point it started to dawn on me that other agendas were at play - agendas I really needed to work out. I know it's wrong to make snap judgements, but sometimes you just have to heed your instincts. I had viewed casimir2 as untrustworthy from the start. What I needed to do was work out *why*. Quickly. But I couldn't.

Ollie raised the rifle and steadied it. Everyone's nerves were fraying by the second. After what seemed like an eternity, casimir2 sneered, "You won't use it and you know it… you know it, you coward!"

I shook my head. "It's probably not a good idea to taunt someone aiming a rifle at you," I warned.

I noticed Ollie was breathing heavily, and his hand was shaking violently. "Get in the ship!" he commanded.

Casimir2 ignored him. "I'm staying here," he insisted. Turning away from us, he started lugging a box of equipment he had retrieved earlier. "You can take the extricator. I'm staying… I'm staying to repair the cruiser. I'll follow later."

"Ollie, you have to get back," I said, concerned about his evident debility.

"I'm not leavin' 'im 'ere!" said Ollie, now using the weapon as a support to keep his balance.

"You go on ahead, Ollie," I told him. "I'll stay with this guy. You *must* get back while you still can."

"Don't trust 'im with anythin'!" Ollie snarled, thrusting the laser weapon into my hands. "'E's your prisoner - see that it stays that way! And under no circumstances let 'im take you to the gateway complex."

"Huh? What's the gateway complex?" I asked. I had no idea what he was talking about.

"The worm'ole gateway. The place where you came

in," said Ollie tetchily. Panting hard, he turned and climbed unsteadily into the extricator vehicle. After an agonisingly long pause, in which I could sense him struggling with the controls, the ship hummed louder and took off, sending clouds of fine sand towards us.

"How did he learn to fly that thing?" I asked.

"The controls are intuitive, even for you erflings," said casimir2, frowning at the ship's flight pattern as it receded erratically into the distance.

"That," I observed, "is the flight pattern of a bumble bee.... with hiccups."

"What *is* he doing?" casimir2 grumbled, "It's intuitive, I tell you... intuitive. Maybe he's sneezing or, yeah, hiccups. How can anyone not operate a series one landstar erutus? You know what? It's his feet... his feet! I noticed it earlier – his feet are huge!"

A particularly large plume of dust erupted on the horizon, rising inexorably until it detached itself and left a smudge on the sky.

"Doesn't look like the stopping bit is very intuitive," I fretted. "I hope he's okay."

. . .

Casimir2 was eyeing the weapon in my hands. Muttering something under his breath, he looked away. I tested the weight of the rifle and gingerly slid my hand away from the trigger. A horrible feeling tingled down my neck and seeped into the pit of my stomach as it dawned on me that Ollie had subtly but profoundly changed the entire dynamic of my visit to the planet. He had critically jeopardised my position. Hell, he had blown away any credibility I might have had as an intermediary. An honest broker and neutral peacemaker would not be pointing a rifle at one of the key figures in the dispute between the Mortians and the nefeshchaya earthlings.

. . .

Casimir2's efforts at repairing the cruiser were about as effective as tackling a crocodile with a fly swatter. For some reason, he'd insisted on us spending over half an hour turning the thing onto its back. Once we'd achieved it, he set to work tentatively dusting the underside with something resembling a loo brush. He might as well have been scratching its belly as it lay there as helpless as a turtle on its back.

Finally, exasperated, I put it to him: "You don't actually know how to fix it, do you?"

"You erflings! I'm getting rather fed up… fed up

with your negative attitude!"

"Yeah, well, I'm getting rather fed up with the lack of breakfast."

"Your grandmother made a great impression when she visited us… a great impression. I expected you to be more resourceful. If your grandmother was here… if she was here and needed breakfast, she would have gone off to pick mushrooms."

"You have mushrooms here?"

"No," said casimir2. "That's not the point… not the point. The point is to be resourceful." He bent down to pull something out of the sand and thrust it at me. "Here, eat this!"

"What? No! No way."

"Why?" His sneer resembled a dog's hind leg. "Because it doesn't have hollandaise sauce? Because… because there's no ketchup?"

"No," I replied. "Because it's a small shrub."

I didn't find him at all engaging, but I admit I was impressed by his thorough knowledge of human culture on Earth. I was aware, obviously, through my grandmother, that Mortians had carried out extensive studies of our behaviour and interactions for several decades. When I mentioned this, he relished the opportunity to boast about his particular special interest in linguistics. "Why, yes," he told me with a slightly superior smile, "I'm an authority on erfling colloquialism and art. I studied the two subjects in tandem."

I thought to ask why, but I didn't.

"Yeah," he said. "I know shedloads of stuff about art on Erf."

"Erf?"

"Yeah," said casimir2, resuming his ineffectual dusting. "Ask me about Lenny… Lenny da Vinci."

"It's Leonardo," I pointed out pedantically.

"So, ask me about Leonardy da Vinci."

I cringed, unsure if I was irritated or infuriated or both. "It's not Leonardy! It's Leonardo! L-e-o-n-a-r-d-o!"

Casimir2 paused his dusting and shrugged. "Okay, well, ask me… ask me about Banksy."

It was obviously not possible to run off in all directions at the same time, but, if it had been, I'd have done it. That's how exasperated I was. "Is that it?" I asked. "Are you just going to *dust* that thing?"

"Always works," he confirmed.

This went on for some time and I was nearing the end of my tether. Actually, my tether had snapped some time ago. "How long have I known you?" I asked him.

Without looking up from his dusting, he said, "Not long... not long. Three days. Why?"

"Well, it's not working out," I said sardonically, trying to retain my sense of humour. "If you weren't my prisoner, I'd suggest that maybe we need a few days apart. Anyway, if you don't get this thing fixed in two minutes, we're going to start walking. I'm worried about Ollie."

"Your erfling empathy is a waste of energy," he said, dismissively. "Empathy represses analytic thought. And vice versa. We need to focus... we need to focus on repairing the cruiser."

"Well, can't you call for someone else? Don't you have a guy who understands these cruiser things?"

"A mechanic?"

"Yes," I said. "A mechanic. Someone who can do more than just wave a duster at it."

"We have a badass expert... expert mechanic."

"Well, call him on your microwocky thing! Get him over here!"

"I can't," said casimir2, his voice sinking.

"Why not?"

"I owe him... I owe him money."

"Well, speak to someone else!" I insisted.

He tapped away at his microwocky and said, "Hello?"

The unmistakable sound of yukawa3's dulcet honking voice replied, "Hello. You've reached emergency response services. What is your emergency? To ensure better customer service, this transmission may be monitored."

Casimir2 shrugged. "It's a recording," he explained.

Heat waves appeared to flicker above the ground before radiating up towards the sky. I was vaguely aware that I'd travelled east from nefeshchaya, but the twin suns were now nearing their zeniths and they would provide no real clue as to which way was west, so I abandoned the idea of walking. Stretching out on the sand, I propped myself by my elbows and watched casimir2 listlessly dusting the underside of the cruiser. Clearly, Mortians had a fluid concept of time, one in which urgency was considered a pointless and foolish construct. Even as that thought was taking hold in my mind, I recalled the first words I'd heard polkingbeal67 speak – he'd been encouraging his comrades to act fast, uttering some gibberish about tomorrow being yesterday two days from now. I started to wonder if casimir2 was purposely detaining me for some reason.

"Come to think of it," I said probingly, "can't you use your microwocky to fix the cruiser? Can't it at least tell you what to do?"

Casimir2 shrugged. "It tells me to dust… to dust the electromagnetic propulsion drives."

"Show me!" I insisted, levering myself back to my feet.

"I can't."

"Why not?"

"Well, it's not working… not working at the moment," he said, evasively.

"But I thought it was like the most genius piece of technology ever seen," I baited him.

"It is," he countered. "But it has one critical flaw."

"What's that?"

"Battery… battery life."

"Really? Is that what you're going with?" By now, I

was fairly sure he was deliberately procrastinating. But what could I do about it?

COMPOS MENTIS

Once we'd got the cruiser upright, we climbed in and verified that everything was functioning normally. Obviously, I decided it would be injudicious to part with the weapon, so I allowed casimir2 to take the controls. He glanced warily across at me, then back at the tiller and we sped off, sand and dust billowing behind us like the wake of a speedboat.

"We're going back to nefeshchaya, right?" I asked.

Casimir2 glanced at me again and nodded.

As I settled back and observed the landscape, I figured out that we were travelling *away* from nefeshchaya. For one thing, the cruiser hadn't changed its orientation at any point and, for another thing, the afternoon shadows were pointing east. Well, at least it proved I had been right to distrust casimir2. Then I realised I didn't *want* to be right.

Agitated, I wiped my clammy hands on my tunic, picked up the rifle, raised it and then placed it in my lap again. Faced with the prospect of a fight, my usual strategies involved cracking a joke or acting as pathetic as possible or running away from the scene. People say I wouldn't say boo to a goose. But then, why *would* I? A goose can give you quite a nip on the back of the leg. Could I envisage myself wielding a weapon in a way that casimir2 might possibly take me seriously? Suddenly, the whole situation was fraught with difficulty, danger and unforeseeable consequences. Bizarrely, it also occurred to me that I hadn't been to a barbecue in ages. You know, it's weird how your brain does that kind of thing when you're under stress - how it takes refuge in comforting thoughts to protect you from the more disturbing stuff. I figured the more I learned about extra-terrestrial life, the better I liked barbecues.

What would they have had me do, I wondered, if I could have got through to Mission Control at Houston? Not that NASA had anything to do with any of this, apart from sending the Voyager space probes into space all those years ago! If I'd had a metaphorical angel and a metaphorical devil sitting on my shoulders, I wondered what they would have been saying. And I wondered which one of them I should have been listening to. It's lucky I wasn't being paid to think. Come to think of it, I wasn't being paid at all. And that certainly focuses the mind, right? No, not really. Nothing could have helped me focus my mind at that moment, so I just sat there trying to look as cool and badass as possible, while casimir2 drove the cruiser across the plains, past an assortment of eerie, glimmering methane lakes, huge clouds of vapour hanging in the air above most of them.

Eventually, I decided I had no option but to challenge him.

"Where are we going?" I asked. "I'm well aware we're *not* heading back towards nefeshchaya. You're taking me to the gateway complex, aren't you?"

"Oh, why... why would I do that?" he asked, his eyes avoiding mine.

"I don't know," I replied. "Maybe because your leader has ordered you to send me back to Earth?" It was a reasonable assumption, based on what he had told me previously. But, of course, I *couldn't* be sent back, because of the heart surgery.

Weaving the cruiser around a cluster of rock outcrops, he nodded slowly and said, "Yes... yes, he has ordered me to send you back." Applying the reverse thrusters, he waited till the cruiser rocked to a halt. "Don't you *want* to go back?"

I had to think about that. I had to think about that with all the intensity of my soul. I was confused. Confused on all sorts of levels. Was I missing something? Was there some way I *could* safely return home? No, I knew that wasn't possible really. I tried to read his face, tried to discover, in those inscrutable bulging eyes set close to the sides of his face, some hidden clue to his real intent. I should have challenged him outright, but I didn't. "Yeah, of course," I mumbled. "I want to go back, if that's possible. There's some stuff I need to sort out first, but, yeah, I'd like to return eventually."

"What stuff do you need to sort out?"

"I was brought here to act as a peace ambassador for Earth," I explained. "I want to help pave the way for peaceful relations between our two planets and I want to help the nefeshchayan people return to their ancestral homeland."

I fancy a sly look came over his face. "What if I were to give you my assurance… my personal assurance that the nefeshchayans *will* be returned to Earth? And what if I were to tell you that we are now committed to establishing harmonious relations… harmonious relations with *all* humanoids in the known universe?"

Ignoring the altruistic claptrap, I asked him: "You can do that? You're prepared to send them to Earth? Why didn't polkingbeal67 tell me this?"

Casimir2 delivered a detailed insight into the

Mortian leader's deteriorating health and mental state, his erratic decision-making and his tempestuous behaviour. "I'm sure you understand where I'm going with this," he said.

I nodded. "Yes, definitely. I suppose so. No, I don't understand. What are you saying?" I demanded. "Do you intend to replace him?"

He didn't answer, but I caught the devious glint in his eyes. "And what about *your* situation?" he inquired. "Wouldn't you like to go back... go back to Earth? Don't you want to be with... with what's her name? Aysha? Wouldn't you like to see her again?"

"Yes, of course, but..." A thousand thoughts cascaded through my brain like dominoes toppling in a graceful arc. Except it wasn't a graceful arc – the unravelling of my thoughts was about as graceful as a camel on roller skates. What about the implications of the surgery he'd carried out on me? Obviously, he knew that I wouldn't survive if I returned to Earth. But perhaps he didn't realise that *I* knew that. Well, whether he realised it or not, it would appear that he intended to kill me. Was this the moment when I was supposed to say, 'you'll never get away with this'?

"You miss Aysha, right?" he asked, touching a very tender nerve. "So, why wait?"

Getting distracted and struggling to retain focus, I blinked hard. It probably wasn't the most effectual response, but, hey, blinking helps to keep your eyes nourished and well-lubricated. "So the nefeshchayans will be sent home to Earth?" I asked.

"I can give you certain assurances," he repeated. "You can trust me. It's a... it's a bona fide offer."

Those words touched another tender nerve. Not because I was being asked to trust such a weasel, but because he threw in a Latin phrase – a phrase that rang more alarm bells for me than a fire station on a busy day. Back on Earth, yukawa3 had told me that the increasing use of Latin words and phrases was a clear indication that a person's brain had been infiltrated by chilloks.

I must explain. You may recall me mentioning the chilloks before? Highly developed, diminutive creatures evolved from ants. Well, I need to tell you more about them. For one thing, it's important to grasp that the successful perpetuation of the chillok species depended entirely on a telepathic networking capability that had evolved on a colossal multi-universe scale. A critical component of that capability was the proliferation of a chillok sub-family known as cerebrum ambulans, elusive microbe-sized creatures that invaded humanoid skulls and manipulated the host's brain function, a process the Mortians referred to as 'brain tuning'. The early signs and symptoms of this foreign incursion in the brain could be difficult to spot, but a penchant for speaking Latin offered a tell-tale clue.

I was reeling with an overload of fresh doubts, a whole new raft of preposterous dilemmas. If my brain had had a rev counter, the needle would have been pegged in the red zone. In the short term, I needed to give myself some time to think. I blurted out the most discomposing question I could think of: "Why was there a penguin in the bar where you're being held prisoners?" I'd been meaning to ask this for some time, in any case.

"A penguin?"

"In the bar. The one with the golf mural. I swear there was a penguin in the bar when I was talking to polkingbeal67."

"Oh, no, no, no," said casimir2. "That was... that was yukawa3."

"Right," I said dubiously. "Mm-hmm. Well, it looked a lot like a penguin. It turned its head a lot like a penguin. It walked a lot like a penguin. So, honestly, unless you guys are like the best penguin impersonators of all time..."

Casimir2 fiddled with various buttons and levers on the control panel. "I wouldn't lie to you."

"You wouldn't?"

"Never, as long as we both shall live," he assured me. "It was yukawa3. You're aware… you're aware that we have the ability to acquire different physical forms? We have developed a biomimetic mutator that enables us to transform… to transform our appearances."

I was tempted to ask why, therefore, he persisted with his current hideous anatomy, but I restrained myself and simply nodded.

He shrugged. "All I'm saying is - it's not unusual… not unusual for us to adopt different appearances."

I wasn't buying that. "You're saying yukawa3 turned into a penguin because you have a kind of casual dress code? And so he thought he'd embrace his inner penguin?"

"Kind of," said casimir2, chuckling with all the sincerity of a cat claiming innocence while holding a bird carcass in its mouth. "Like, why fit in… why fit in when you were born to be a penguin? Eh?"

I shot him a look that I might have reserved for someone who interrupted me while I was listening to one of my favourite northern soul songs.

"Okay, I'll level with you," he said. "I'll explain properly. He was being punished... punished, you see? Our revered leader was displeased with him."

"How is it a punishment to be a penguin?"

"Well, for one thing, there are no fish on this planet," said casimir2. "And, for another thing, yukawa3 has an aversion... an aversion to being a penguin."

I knew that was true – yukawa3 had told me as much when we were back on Earth. By this time, the penguin thing was seriously distracting me from contemplating a possible chillok incursion into casimir2's brain. What I couldn't understand was why, assuming the chilloks were planning another attempt at invasion, they would waste so much time and energy on *me*. Surely, they had bigger fish to fry? Fish. Penguin. I was getting everything massively confused. "If he doesn't like being a penguin, why can't he just transform himself back again?" I asked.

Lines of figures scrolled on the monitor as casimir2 watched intently, knobbly finger poised above a silver switch. "His mutator was confiscated," he explained. "Don't worry... don't worry about him. He'll be fine."

"He can't eat!" I objected, fixing casimir2 with my

patented glare, the one that would annihilate a whole bunch of neighbourhood cats back home in my garden. It was pretty scary.

But it made no impression on him at all. "It's only a temporary punishment," he shrugged. "A short sharp shock. Now, have you made up your mind about… about going home? In just ten of your Earth minutes, you could be flying… flying through a wormhole and then arriving back on terra firma with Aysha."

The slyness in his voice made me bristle, and the Latin phrase struck me like a blow to the belly.

"Okay," he said with a studied indifference. "Where do you want me to drive you? Nefeshchaya or… or the gateway complex, where I can send you happily on your way back to Aysha?"

Clearly, he was extremely keen to get rid of me. But I couldn't fathom why I represented such a threat. Furthermore, I was struggling to understand who my enemy really was. Which scenario was the most plausible? Was I a threat to casimir2 and his ambitions to oust polkingbeal67 and become the Mortian leader? Or did I pose a threat to the chilloks in their quest for planetary domination? Or, indeed, both? I needed to buy more time to think. I cleared my throat and asked, "Who decided on the punishment? Surely not polkingbeal67?"

"Why not?"

"It was *you*, wasn't it?" I accused, becoming less inhibited in my handling of this devious character.

Affecting an aura of nonchalance, he replied in a deadpan voice: "Yes, but I was acting in the interests of our leader... our ailing revered leader."

"In what way?" I asked.

"Yukawa3's conduct deserved some form of censure as... as a mark of our revered leader's disapproval." He puckered his lips into something resembling a duck's bill. "And I duly obliged."

"Why *you*?"

"I had first dibs," he replied.

While he launched into a tirade of invective against polkingbeal67 and his perceived shortcomings, I did some more thinking. Digging deep in my memory, I recalled the stuff yukawa3 had told me about the cerebra ambulans. He'd described them as microbe entities that implanted themselves in people's brains with a view to inducing a kind of mass hypnosis. (Apparently, they'd even infiltrated *yukawa3's* brain – he claimed it was one of the greatest challenges they'd ever come across!) Acting like a kind of virus, the collective psychosis would have had the effect of making everyone on Earth depressed to the point of self-destruction. According to Aysha's friend, Disney, what yukawa3 had been describing was similar to what Native American people used to call 'wetiko'. Disney knew all kinds of esoteric stuff like that.

And it would have been the perfect crime – homo sapiens on Earth would have been wiped out, and the intergalactic courts would have had no reason to suspect the chilloks.

The whole scheme had been abandoned when Disney's sister, Hinton, had responded positively to an antidote yukawa3 had obtained from his home planet. The chilloks simply appeared to give up on the whole thing.

I don't know how long it took me to think all that stuff, but it was like at least ten or fifteen minutes. And casimir2 still had his teeth into polkingbeal67 like a terrier at a trouser leg. So I told him "That's enough already!" and gave him a half-hearted slap on the arm. The shriek he uttered was simply terrible to hear.

"I hardly touched you!" I snorted. "That's pathetic. It was nothing more than the tiniest slap."

"Is it pathetic to suffer… to suffer the most severe trauma ever experienced… ever experienced by any Mortian ever in the history of the universe?" he wailed, licking his arm like a child licking an ice cream cone. "That's pain... that's pain with a capital 'P'."

"Even if it's in the middle of a sentence?" I queried, tongue in cheek.

"You don't understand... you don't understand Mortian pain!"

"What's so special about *Mortian* pain?"

"It's special because we seldom experience it," he said. "So, if we encounter it, it comes as a total shock. It's like your belly is turning inside out and trying... trying to slither out of your throat."

"You mean like belching?" I asked, frivolously.

"We have highly evolved rational minds and we've learned to dismiss pain immediately, as soon as our brains have processed the threat. Which is usually... immediately."

I recalled yukawa3 not reacting to a kick in the back, when we'd first arrived. "So, what happened? Surely it was obvious that me tapping you on the arm didn't represent any kind of threat?"

"I wasn't *ready*!" he pouted, sulking like a pig in an abattoir. "I have to process it. Wait till I'm *ready*... wait till I'm *ready* next time!"

"So... have you processed it yet?" I asked, flicking a finger at his arm once more, barely able to contain my amusement.

He waved his hand in a gesture of dismissal. "Of course! Pah! That was... that was nothing. Punch me, if you like! If I know it's coming, I'll feel absolutely nothing... absolutely nothing at all."

Tempted as I was to accept the invitation, I decided the less direct contact I had with his loathsome skin the better.

"Let's go find some blanids!" he urged, quickly recovering his mettle.

"Why?"

"I could let one of them spit... spit in my eye! I wouldn't feel a thing!" he boasted with an air of smug bravado.

"What good would that do anybody?" I asked.

"That would do a *lot* of good!" he insisted. "I would pretend to be harmed and it would help... it would help the blanid look tough... look tough in front of his blanid friends. And it wouldn't hurt me at all and we'd laugh and we'd all feel happy."

While casimir2 went through a range of facial expressions that put me in mind of a badly overacted pantomime villain, I reflected on yukawa3's explanation for the chilloks' aborted invasion. I must warn you that this is not easy to comprehend. I implore you to read it at least three times (it took me three attempts to write it).

Firstly, it's worth considering the chilloks' earlier attempt to invade Melinda (it had been known as Smolin9 at the time). On that occasion, they had been thwarted when polkingbeal67 delivered a genuinely heartfelt treatise on friendship and reconciliation and the sanctity of life and pan-galactic respect. This was atypical behaviour for a Mortian. According to expert analysis, the cerebra ambulans had been so alarmed by the heady cocktail of brain chemicals swishing around in polkingbeal67's brain that they just gave up and withdrew!

For me to convey to you why certain brain chemicals caused the chilloks so much grief, I need to tell you all I know about neurotransmitters. Don't worry – that won't take long!

Well, basically, certain neurotransmitters like serotonin, dopamine, oxytocin and endorphins are chemicals that determine our moods and our sense of well-being. You probably know that, but what you may *not* know is the process by which these chemicals interact and communicate. They do this by means of biological junctions known as synapses.

One thing that's particularly relevant here is reuptake - the process by which the 'happy' chemicals are reabsorbed after they've performed their synaptic activity. When yukawa3 visited me on Earth, he explained that all neurotransmitters contain a key amino acid called 'hartglue'. Typically, Mortian brains had an abundance of hartglue but were deficient in other 'happy' chemicals. The reverse was true of us earthlings. Earthling scientists were unaware of hartglue at the time. They were also unaware that we had become progressively deficient in it. And this deficiency had upset the metabolism of neurotransmitters to the point where reuptake and synaptic activity were jeopardised. In short, the brain's 'happy' chemicals had simply started to disappear!

The prospective invasion of Earth by the chilloks was essentially defeated when yukawa3 obtained some hartglue from Smolin9/Melinda and administered it to Hinton, who had been targeted by the chillok brain tuners. It transpired that this totally compromised the chilloks' ability to achieve effective brain tuning.

Essentially, cerebrum ambulans - the key chillok sub-family – could not co-exist with any species blessed with a good balance of 'happy' chemicals. And a declining cerebrum ambulans sub-family effectively destabilised the entire network communication system that was so essential to the chilloks' success.

The Mortians believed that the chillok threat had been eliminated on both Melinda and Earth, but I was now starting to have my doubts. What if the chilloks had *not* abandoned invasion plans in respect of either planet. What if the earlier incursions had been nothing more than trials? What if they'd just been conducting some initial research?

"What if I just take you to the gateway complex and we try to make contact… make contact with Aysha?" Casimir2's eyes gleamed with mischief as he spoke. "I can set up… set up a wormhole communication channel."

"Okay," I said in an unguarded, knee-jerk moment. Coming to my senses, I added, "But first I must speak to polkingbeal67. Take me to your leader." I really wished I hadn't said that. I recalled Aysha's joke about clichés being such old hat.

For what it was worth, I made a small movement of my hand towards the rifle.

ANOTHER BAR, ANOTHER BRAWL

We passed the wreck of the landstar erutus extricator ship and I insisted that we stop to check. I was pretty sure Ollie must have got out and walked the rest of the way to nefeshchaya – it wasn't too far away. But I wanted to be absolutely sure. The upturned hull was partially submerged in sand. Wisps of smoke, like the breath of dragons, continued to rise from various vents and the landing gear hinges. "How had it overturned?" I wondered. My heart was sinking like a sack of cement as it dawned on me that Ollie may still have been trapped inside.

Casimir2 was reluctant to open the gull-wing doors. "May his journey through life be filled… filled with happiness," he said.

"What?" I asked in a shaky voice.

"May his obstacles be few… few and far between," he continued in cloying insincerity. "May he always feel loved… loved and secure. We come together as a family and a community and we make our pledge to raise him spiritually. Ad vitam aeternum."

Shuddering at the implications of his use of Latin, I now realised he was attempting to deliver some kind of eulogy for Ollie. "I think you'll find those words are for a christening," I pointed out. Clearly, casimir2's research into earthling culture was at best confused and at worst seriously flawed.

One thing was obvious – there was no way we could possibly have dug our way through to Ollie without special equipment. I was about to tell casimir2 to move on, when something collided with the windscreen. The loud ping startled both of us.

"Orbis... orbis bird," said casimir2, dismissively.

Before I could reply, there was another loud pop and the windscreen trembled. A bird with something small and red in its beak stared at us as it balanced precariously on the lip of the windscreen. It wasn't an orbis bird. "Pigeon," I observed.

The bird began to tap at the windscreen with the object in its beak, slowly at first, then more insistently.

"It's a button," I said. "A red button." Suddenly, it dawned on me that it was a button from Ollie's tunic. "Open the doors!" I commanded, "And get out! Quickly!" I suppose I just didn't want to give casimir2 the opportunity of driving off without me. Taking his arm, I walked around the wreck, surveying the scene and looking for other traces of clothing. Something in the distance caught my eye. It was Ollie.

He was alive, but apparently unconscious.

"How many fingers am I holding up?" I asked him. I'm afraid my first aid knowledge extended no further than this. In any event, he was very evidently unconscious. Obviously, he'd either been thrown clear, or he'd managed to dig his way out after the crash and had attempted to walk for help. We grasped an arm apiece and, with great difficulty, carried him to the cruiser, his heels dragging through the sand. His breathing was laboured. After propping him up as best we could in the passenger seat, casimir2 and I exchanged meaningful glances. Clearly, there wasn't enough room for all of us to travel in the cruiser.

"I'll come back for you as soon as I can," I assured him with something approaching a polite smile.

He kind of snarled at me and said, "Best of luck... best of luck with your future endeavours!"

I had no idea what that meant, and I didn't have time to give it much thought. I wondered if I should tie him to a tree. But there wasn't one. "If you stay here, I'll be right back," I promised, closing the doors and firing the forward thrusters.

. . .

As John and the woman with the skull tattoo tended to the patient, I arranged for casimir2 to be picked up, and I negotiated an interview with polkingbeal67.

Having been escorted by two nefeshchayan guards to the Irish bar that doubled as a makeshift prison for the Mortians, I immediately spotted the penguin with the yellow sou'wester waddling back and forth on the carpeted floor at the far end of the golf mural. Turning to polkingbeal67, I came right out and asked, "Is that yukawa3?"

Polkingbeal67 lifted a piece of seaweed and peered at it. "You already know the answer to the questions lingering inside your head," he said.

"He's being punished?"

"It would appear so," said polkingbeal67, waving the seaweed and following it with his uncovered eye.

"So, why?" I asked, shaking my head. "Why are you punishing him?"

"Not me," he responded with a shrug. "But it doesn't matter. It's amazing how much good you can do if you don't care who gets the credit."

"I want to speak to him," I said. "It's important. Only, you'll have to release him from the penguin suit thing. I don't speak penguinese."

With an airy wave of his hand, polkingbeal67 indicated the mutator on the small high table near the bar.

"What do I do?" I asked, exploring it tentatively with my fingers.

Polkingbeal67 was about as helpful as a wooden magnet. "Press cancel?" he suggested. "I don't know. I haven't used one of those for eons."

"So, you don't adopt other identities?"

"I don't need to," he replied. "I simply find another spirit hiding inside me and I let that spirit run free. There are no limitations to the mind except those that we acknowledge."

"That's very deep, but I don't think it's going to help this penguin very much," I said.

One of the other Mortians came forward, bowed courteously and took the mutator from me. "Excuse me," he said deferentially. "Please allow me to introduce myself. I am nipkow4."

"Do you know how to operate this thing?" I asked him. "Oh, yeah, and how do you do?"

Without replying, he held the device at arm's length in his right hand. Then, standing on one leg like a flamingo, he extended his left arm above his head. "I have one leg slightly shorter than the other," he explained. "We need to be perfectly balanced to execute this correctly."

The penguin raised a flipper and prodded nipkow4 with it.

"No, don't do that!" warned nipkow4, teetering slightly. "Nothing can be unstable or off-balance when you use a mutator!" He looked about as stable as a cow on a tightrope, especially when he extended his leg like a dog at a lamppost. It occurred to me that his uncoordinated ballerina pose couldn't possibly have been an improvement on his natural body asymmetry, but the point became a purely academic one anyway when the penguin slapped nipkow4's standing leg, sending him careering across the floor. He ended up straddled over a card table, peanut shells scattered all around him.

"Wouldn't it be the *penguin* that needs to be balanced?" I ventured tentatively. The penguin nodded and spread his flippers apart as if to say, "That's what I was trying to tell him!"

The metamorphosis, when it finally took place, was slow and gradual like a tortoise making a handbrake turn. He was tall for a Mortian. As tall as a giraffe. Well, you know, a five-foot-one-inch giraffe. Having recovered his natural form, yukawa3 blew out his cheeks, smacked his lips and made a strange bubbling noise. "Well if you think that was a heinous thing to do to a sentient being, it was," he said in a curiously high-pitched voice, slurring his S's and wobbling from one leg to the other. The yellow sou'wester looked even more ridiculous on his head than it did before.

"A sentient being?" cackled casimir2, who suddenly appeared at the door, wrenching himself free from the loosened grip of the two nefeshchayans who had retrieved him from the crash site. "Well, that's a bit… that's a bit rich."

I wasn't sure at first why he was speaking in English, but then he turned and fixed me with a withering gaze like a tractor beam. I almost had to clutch the side of a table to resist being sucked towards him. "This erfling held me at gunpoint and should not be trusted in any circumstances. Who ordered the discontinuation of yukawa3's punishment?"

An involuntary guttural pop escaped polkingbeal67's throat and he raised his arms as if appealing to a divine power. "I'd like to help you out," he said, addressing casimir2.

Casimir2 turned his gaze onto the planetary leader and said with a sinister grin on his lips, "Help me out? *You… you* want to help *me* out?"

"Yes, I'd like to help you out," repeated polkingbeal67, furling and unfurling his umbrella in desultory fashion. "If you want happiness for a lifetime, help someone else out. Now then, which way did you come in?"

The stares they exchanged were colder than a polar bear's nose. In the blink of an eye, they were at one another's throats like stray cats contesting a discarded fish tail, punching, kicking, eye-gouging and headbutting. The umbrella hit the floor at my feet, and I used it to pry them apart – I was reluctant to use my hands on casimir2's rubbery, carbuncular, oozing skin. That didn't work, so I threw a jug of greenish liquid at him. Eventually, a couple of the Mortians came to my assistance and an uneasy calm prevailed. Casimir2's posture was rigid, and he had clenched his jaw tight. I figured that whatever was eating him up inside, it probably wasn't enjoying the experience.

It was yukawa3 who broke the silence. "We need answers," he said with a look of unyielding intensity quite at odds with the rest of his thin, fragile appearance and cagey expression.

"Answers to what?" said casimir2.

"Answers to the questions," yukawa3 answered, affecting an enigmatic air that hinted just slightly at a depth of insight that simply wasn't there.

"You have some questions?" polkingbeal67 enquired, reclaiming his umbrella.

Yukawa3 was unprepared for any direct responses. Or any responses at all, actually. "Not *my* questions," he said. "*Other* people's questions."

Casimir2 brushed him aside with a peremptory wave of his scabrous hand. "Go away!" he said. "Go... go away, before we turn you back into a penguin!" He plucked the sou'wester from yukawa3's head and tossed it across the room.

Tension filled the air like the smell of sour milk that someone left in a van overnight during a heatwave. Nipkow4 started picking up the crushed peanut shells. Polkingbeal67 scowled at the umbrella as if it were responsible for all his woes. Deciding that that was indeed the case, he flung the offending object into the corner of the room in disgust.

It seemed as if the apogee of Mortian civilisation had suddenly suffered a debilitating attack of vertigo and become utterly paralysed. And, frankly, I didn't know if I should help them out or clear off and just leave them to it.

And there we have it, people of Earth. There's absolutely no need to look upon advanced alien civilisations in wonder and reverence. Ultimately, their behaviour lapses into a predictably dysfunctional dynamic just as it does on our own planet. Same old, same old. At the other end of the universe, behind a door labelled "Private Bar", there are no great secrets of human existence – it's just another bar, another brawl.

THE QUANDARY

Ensconced together in a corner of the bar, yukawa3 and I attempted to piece together the events of the last couple of days.

"It would be a direct violation of intergalactic protocol," said yukawa3, "to send the nefeshchayans back to Earth right now. I hope that answers your question."

"What question?" I asked. "I never asked a question. Why would it be a violation of... whatever you said?"

"Well, *that*'s a question, isn't it? And the answer is... because you're not allowed to do things like that without an assessment of all the factors." He puckered his lips and softly blew air from them. "It is spoken," he added.

"*What* is spoken?" I asked "And by whom? And what factors?"

"See?" said yukawa3. "I tried to tell people we needed answers to questions."

"You weren't talking about *those* questions, though, were you?" I said, becoming bored and irritated.

Yukawa3 nodded sagely (at least, he probably thought it was sagely). "No question about it."

"Put it this way," I said, after a moment's pause. "Is there any logistical reason why we can't send the nefeshchayans through a wormhole to planet Earth? Any *logistical* reason."

Obviously, I was perfectly aware there *were* problems – serious, palpable problems, such as the daunting impact it would have on the people of Earth if and when alien abductees were suddenly returned out of the blue. Issues surrounding the rehabilitation of the nefeshchayans were certainly challenging. But I wanted to be reassured that there weren't going to be any complications in respect of the wormhole transportation itself.

"I don't know," said yukawa3, fidgeting nervously in his chair.

"What do you mean, you don't know?" I said. "*Can* you send them to Earth? Or not?"

"That's a technical question," he said, steepling his spindly fingers while his eyes darted shiftily at me back and forth. "You'd have to ask casimir2."

"Why?" I asked, with some concern in my voice. "Wait, how many of you are trained and competent to do the wormhole portal thing that casimir2 does?

How many?"

Instead of replying, he rolled his eyes up and stared at the ceiling with intense concentration.

A pang of realisation descended upon me like a solitary locust scouting ahead of the main swarm. "You're kidding, right?"

Yukawa3 shifted in his chair and avoided making eye contact. "If you think wormhole travel is an incredibly complicated realm of science, well, it is," he said. "You know what? If you could meet the person who first discovered a wormhole, wouldn't you like to shake him by the hand?"

"Right now, I'd like to shake you by the throat!" I barked gruffly. "Are you telling me casimir2 is the only person who can transport anyone off this planet?"

Yukawa3 wittered on with studied insouciance. "The first Mortian to discover a stable wormhole was actually one of polkingbeal67's ancestors - a brilliant astrophysicist named polkingbeal53. But I suppose you could shake hands with…"

"I don't want to shake hands with anyone!" I interrupted brusquely, fixing him with an icy stare.

"Well, you can't anyway," said yukawa3. "Because, although polkingbeal53 was the first *Mortian* to discover a wormhole, he was beaten to it by the chilloks."

That was certainly intriguing. "The first person to discover a wormhole was an *ant*?" I said incredulously. Thinking about it, I had absolutely no reason to be sceptical – yukawa3 had told me before that the microstructure of chillok brain tissue surpassed by millions of times the entire genetic sequence of human DNA.

"Well, would you have been happier if it had been, you know, a worm?" he retorted airily. That was weird. Yukawa3 never did sarcasm. "Wormhole travel - that's what ants, I mean chilloks, are especially famous for."

"Right," I said, abandoning the need for further elucidation. And there was me thinking ants were only responsible for things like helping diseases thrive. "Well, let's face it, they could have done a better job," I added. "Discovering wormhole travel deserves a bit of credit, I guess. But they missed out big time. There are no timetables, no bureaux de change, no newsagents or cafes, no WiFi, no flight attendants demonstrating the life jackets and no duty-free shopping. It's a shambles."

I went on to vent all my spleen concerning casimir2 and raised the possibility that the balance of his mind had been compromised by cerebra ambulans.

The two of us then sat in silence for a full minute.

"We need to infiltrate them!" declared yukawa3 in a tone that would have carried conviction, had he not banged his fist for emphasis and caught the lip of an ashtray, sending it hurtling across the table. He bleated like a goat in a tiger's den, as a cloud of old cigarette ash descended onto the carpet.

"Infiltrate who?" I asked.

Yukawa3 looked at me as if I had frogs crawling out of my ears. "Why, the chilloks, of course!" he said.

"*We* need to infiltrate *them*?" I asked derisively. "And how do you propose that we should set about doing that?"

"It's obvious if you think about it," he scoffed. And then his eyes drifted around the room. "Let me think about it."

While he was thinking, I did some thinking of my own. Firstly, I wondered why yukawa3 had immediately made this all about the chilloks. I mean perhaps he was right - perhaps casimir2's normal personality had been totally compromised by the insidious influence of the cerebrum ambulans. But surely, given that there was very little anyone could do about the braintuning antics of these chillok-related creatures, the problem was, to all intents and purposes, effectively centred around casimir2, purely because dealing with *him* represented the only feasible solution available to us. We had very limited means at our disposal to undermine, let alone defeat, the scourge of chillok infiltration. Yes, no question, we had to deal with *him*. With casimir2. What concerned me, quite deeply, when I pondered things, was the complete lack of scrutiny applied to this disreputable, devious character. Setting aside polkingbeal67's scathing assessment of him, casimir2 clearly enjoyed plenty of support from the other Mortians, who appeared to have an overwhelming, almost unquestioning degree of trust in him. Furthermore, I strongly suspected that they endorsed his ambition to wrest power from their current leader. And as much as I disliked polkingbeal67's unpredictable and irrational tendencies, I viewed the alternative as immeasurably worse.

Frankly, I didn't trust casimir2 and I was extremely sceptical of his pledge to despatch the nefeshchayans to Earth without meting out some sort of retribution. And that left me with a quandary: either I took him at his word and advised the nefeshchayans that they could rely on casimir2's sense of honour and integrity (screwy) or I focused on negotiating with polkingbeal67 (phooey!).

I interrupted yukawa3's deep contemplation of the old cigarette stubs scattered upon the table. "I need you to cooperate with me," I told him. "Things are becoming more complicated by the minute, but you brought me here to intercede between polkingbeal67 and my people."

"He has grown old and muddled in his thinking," said yukawa3.

"Yes," I agreed. "But not only that. He doesn't seem to exercise any authority over the rest of you. He believes he's being undermined by casimir2. And I think he's right."

Yukawa3 tilted his head in confusion. "Undermined?" he said. "No, no! Casimir2 is only *guiding* him…"

"Like a devil on his shoulder," I muttered. "Anyway, I want to know who I should be negotiating with. Is it your leader or his, er, guide?"

"Both?" yukawa3 suggested.

Deciding it was time to confront him with all the facts, I looked him straight in the eyes. "Are you aware that casimir2 tried to send me back to Earth?"

"You see?" said yukawa3, grinning as if he'd just won a bet. "He *is* a good guy! He was taking pity on you."

"Yeah," I said. "He was taking pity on me like a good Samaritan hyena helping an injured wildebeest."

"You were probably totally in his face, going on about returning to Earth," said yukawa3 with a dismissive flick of his wrist. "And, let's face it, he could have just ignored you. But he wanted to be the bigger person. That's casimir2 for you - full of apathy and concussion."

"You probably mean empathy and compassion," I advised him, "but you're wrong. Casimir2 meant to kill me."

"What?" Yukawa3's jaw dropped like a clown's trousers without braces.

"I've had the blue blood cell surgery and I would not survive if I returned to Earth."

"Wouldn't you? Oh yeah. But he wouldn't have known that."

"That's not true," I contradicted him. "He knew all right. He knew perfectly well."

"Well, then, that's the chilloks interfering," he explained. "That must be the result of braintuning. Casimir2 is a very clever and good-spirited fellow. The chilloks must have impaired his faculties somehow. So, if you think they're evil and loathsome, well, they are. Between you and me, they could be tunnelling around in any of our brains right now. Including mine. And yours."

Becoming exasperated and exhausted by this argument, I sighed dismissively. "It doesn't make any difference, does it? It doesn't matter who's at home inside that ugly great dome of his, the fact is, he's trying finish me off."

Yukawa3 placed his hand on my arm. "Take my advice," he said. "Go along with whatever casimir2 tells you. He's the smartest one out of all of us. He's obviously got a plan."

My scepticism just grew deeper and deeper. "Why would I take that advice?" I asked him. "It doesn't make any sense."

"You must believe me," he beseeched. "I know about these things. It's a gift I have. I was born at a very early age. Please take my advice."

"Okay," I said. At this point, I'd given up on the prospect of any rational discourse. "I'll take your advice, because you clearly don't want it and you're trying to get rid of it."

"Thank you. You are very wise," he said with obsequious deference. "It is spoken."

"Wait, just one thing," I said, "Do you remember,

when we were back on Earth, you told me that Mortian microwockys can detect the presence of cerebrum ambulans within a radius of five kilometres?"

"Me?" he queried. "I'm afraid you have the wrong yukawa3." For some unaccountable reason, he then put a seat cushion over his head and proceeded to snore. "I'm pretending to be asleep," he hissed, after I prodded him on the arm several times.

"Why?" I asked in amazement.

"You told me you can't wake someone who is pretending to be asleep," he answered in an aggrieved tone.

"Well, for one thing, you might have considered shutting your eyes," I advised him. "And for another, … Never mind. Do you mean you don't want to answer the question?"

"So many questions," he said, swivelling his eyes gravely from side to side.

Impatient and exasperated, I snapped, "Tell me! Can you detect the presence of chilloks or not?"

"Verily," he conceded, "but we've detected them here continuously for many years now."

As I sank into a fog of doom and gloom and despair

about my future, yukawa3 draped a gangly arm around my shoulder and stared into space.

PIGEON OF DISCONTENT

After a restless and uneasy sleep in an improvised bunk that Ollie had set up for me, I breakfasted on something that looked like green scrambled egg drizzled with a bluish oil. Then I took a stroll in the park area. Sitting cross-legged on the ground, I became aware of a pigeon walking around in circles about twelve feet away from me. For some reason, I was captivated by the bird as its head bobbed like a metronome, matching its jerky gait. Every so often, it lifted its head and stared at me with inquisitive eyes.

Thoughts about Aysha returned to torment me. And the betrayal. Naturally, in life there are betrayals and betrayals. I didn't know which category this fell into. I just knew the hurt wouldn't go away. Was it even a betrayal at all? Whatever it was, it had done a fair bit of damage to me. It had left me with an entire crusade of question marks. Question marks that marched in deluded belief towards a promised land that didn't exist. It had left me confused and suffering. And it was a pain no one could help me get through, a pain no one could shield me from, a pain I didn't understand. All I wanted to do now was to stop those relentless question marks - all of them, one by one. Yes, I wanted to know why she'd abandoned me. But I also wanted to know why I was hurting so much.

And yet, deep down inside, I knew these were like yukawa3's questions - questions without answers, because the questions themselves couldn't be properly expressed.

I was in need of some inner peace. I kept trying to tell myself that Aysha's disappearance didn't matter. Nothing significant had changed. Aysha hadn't stopped the suns from rising. She hadn't caused the stars to fall from the sky. Or stopped the clocks. Or made the mountains crumble into the sea. She hadn't stopped my heart beating, even though I was close to wishing that she had. So why did it feel like she *had* done all those things?

I know I'd have been spared all this if she'd never been there in my life and had never made the commitment to travel here with me. But, honestly, I didn't wish that at all. I wouldn't erase any of it, even if I could. In the end, I'd look at it as an experience that helped me grow. Some people enter your life and change your whole direction, so why might it not be the same when people leave? My life simply had to move to a place it might never have gone if Aysha was still in it. Just another change of direction, that's all. God knows, it was careering off in all directions as it was! We'd had the kind of friendship everyone should have. But now it had gone. It had gone, and I don't know why. I guess someday, somehow, I'll be okay with that. But actually, right now, I just wanted the question marks to stop marching, so that I could move on. According to the song, "life is no abyss - somewhere there's a bluebird of happiness."

Okay, well, no sign of a bluebird - I was stuck with a pigeon. And, as I gazed, lost in troubled contemplation, at this pigeon of discontent, it stopped pecking and stood silently. Then it turned its head from side to side and flew off in a flurry of wings as Ollie appeared with a net.

"So help me, I'm going to catch that bird if it's the last thing I ever do!" he grumbled.

"Well, are you guys still ready to launch yourselves unflinchingly into the gaping maw of life on a different planet?" I asked, as Ollie sat across from me and leaned back on his elbows.

"I've no idea what that means," he said. "But if you mean are we still keen to return to Earth, then, yeah, we are. Oh yeah! You bet! First thing I'm gonna do is go fishin'! Well, I'll maybe check up on whatever's left of my family, then I'm 'avin' a beer and goin' fishin'. Hey, do they still eat that spaghetti stuff? Like long twirly bits of string? So, anyway, Neil, thing is, how are the talks going?"

"I'm going to talk to polkingbeal67 later this morning," I assured him. "It's not easy trying to reason with him. I'm not sure I even understand his reluctance to send you all away. On the face of it, he'd just be taking a thorn out of his side. Oh, and, yeah, they still eat spaghetti."

"I guess it's a bit of a tangle," Ollie agreed. "As I understand it, the Mortians get kudos from on 'igh for just 'avin' us 'ere. Y'know, from the Intergalactic Court people? It demonstrates their commitment to a multiculti pluralism agenda. That's what John believes, anyway. The Mortians think everythin' they do is for the benefit of all 'umanity."

"Yeah, that figures."

"So polkingbeal67 is the problem, is 'e?" said Ollie chewing his lip. "Hmm. Well, I've got a brilliant idea! Let's kidnap 'im!" Frowning, he added, "Oh wait, we already 'ave."

A high-pitched, shrill voice rent the air. "Ollie!" Lizzie yelled. "You're on the rota for laundry!"

Ollie rolled his eyes. "Laundry," he muttered. "I ain't got time for domestic chores. I gotta catch and exterminate the pigeons 'fore they take over the entire park."

"There's only one here," I observed.

"Yeah," said Ollie, getting to his feet and picking up his net. "But give 'em a chance and they establish 'emselves before you can say Jack Robinson."

Before he'd said 'Jack Robinson', the pigeon had swooped down and delivered a vicious peck to the crown of Ollie's head. He span around, rubbing the wound. "Well, I'll be a monkey's uncle!" he declared.

Lizzie yelled again and Ollie sloped away. "Fine," he said.

"Wait a minute," I said, hauling myself up off the ground. "Before you go, there's something I wanted to ask you. Did Aysha leave any kind of message for me before she went home?"

Ollie knitted his brows slightly. "Message?" he said. "She didn't have time to leave a message."

"What do you mean? Why not?"

Ollie pushed out his lower lip. "She didn't exactly leave of her own accord, did she?"

I don't know how long it took me to process this,

but Lizzie had called out twice more before I found my tongue. "Huh? I don't get it. What do you mean? She didn't exactly not what? She didn't not leave how?" I blathered in a panicky babble of nonsense and double negatives. "You mean, casimir2 just sent her back and she didn't have any say in the matter?"

"Yeah," he nodded. "That's what happened. I thought you realised that."

I accompanied Ollie to the laundry room, dazed and oblivious to everything going on around me. When he was done with his chores, we went to the bar, the one with the rugby mural, for a light lunch. I've no idea what I ate, but I think it might have been spicy because it made my nose run a bit.

"Are you crying?" asked the woman with the skull tattoo.

Perhaps it wasn't the food after all. In fact, looking down at the table, I realised I hadn't eaten a thing. Tears of pain and rage streamed down my cheeks. My God, what had he done? I jumped up and ran to the toilet, my stomach straining violently with the dry retching. Getting up off my knees and clutching the sides of the sink, I stared at my reflection in the mirror and resolved to kill casimir2 with my bare hands, loath as I was to even contemplate using a barge pole for this purpose.

On returning to the bar, I managed to calm down enough to listen to a conversation between John and Ollie.

"You're talkin' crazy," John asserted. "I'm tellin' you, the reason we could never 'ave spaghetti 'ere is because spaghetti is made from wheat."

"And why the 'ell couldn't we grow wheat?" Ollie asked.

"'Cause there's too much methane in the atmosphere," said John. "Simple as that. But don't worry, when we get to Earth, you can eat spaghetti till it comes out of your ears!"

"You know what?" I said. "You're better off without wheat. We're slaves to wheat on Earth." Obviously, it was a preposterous thing to say, but my rationality had been eroded by extraordinary events.

"Waddya mean 'slaves'?" Ollie shook his head in puzzled fashion.

I leaned back and spewed forth a muddled and bitter diatribe against, well, pretty much everything really, but especially wheat.

"You know it covers millions of square kilometres of the planet's surface?" I asked rhetorically. "About twelve times the size of the land mass you think of as Britain, England, whatever. And how did this treacherous grass thing come to dominate the globe? No? Well, I'll tell you. It did it by exploiting and manipulating us, like cattle. Yep. Cattle."

I was vaguely aware of the dumbfounded expressions gaping at me, but apparently nothing could stop me now. "Day after day, year after year, millennia after millennia – about ninety percent of our entire history, as it happens - we'd been happily hunting and gathering and foraging until some deluded idiot decided to invest more effort in cultivating wheat. The fool! In just a few millennia, there we were: slaves to the devil grass! From dawn till dusk, we did its bidding, breaking our backs clearing fields because wheat didn't like rocks and stones. Then toiling in the scorching hot sun to eliminate its competitors. And why? Because it didn't like to share its space with weeds and other plants that consumed its water and nutrients. I'm telling you it's the grass of the devil!"

Pausing for breath, I noticed that only John and Ollie remained. The others had fled to saner corners of the bar. While the target of my bitterness had been a bit random, I felt a bit better for having vented.

"There may be somethin' in what you say," said Ollie, for no apparent reason other than to make me feel better. "P'rhaps there's more to wheat than meets the eye."

"Too right," I said. I had that tight feeling in the pit of my stomach that I always got when I overreached myself. "It's no coincidence, surely, that the clearest evidence of extra-terrestrial contact we ever used to get on Earth... was crop circles?"

There was no way I could ever recover from such a remark, so I avoided eye contact and fidgeted with a beer mat. Ollie mumbled something and wandered off.

"Did you get answers to my questions?" said John, after a suitable pause. "Did you find out if our safe arrival on Earth can be assured and verified? And, also, 'ow many Mortians are skilled at operating the gateway technology? Those weren't irrelevant questions. I 'ad very good reasons for askin' 'em."

Okay," I said. "Well, as for the second question, I believe it's fair to assume that only casimir2 can operate the technology with any degree of competence."

John shrugged with a sardonic laugh and an air of feigned casualness. "I thought so," he said. "What about verifying the transportation?"

I shook my head.

"You didn't ask 'em?"

"Well, no."

"Are you aware that it's not one 'undred percent reliable? Mistakes 'appen. Accidents 'appen."

"Oh," was all I could manage in reply. I shook my head again.

"Put it this way. We're aware of people – Mortians – who 'ave never turned up where they're s'posed to. Like never!"

"What happens to them?" I had a feeling I was going to regret asking the question.

"Like I said, mistakes and accidents. The way it's been explained to me is – when you enter a worm'ole, your molecular stability goes into flux and all kinds of things can go wrong. You can end up in the wrong place at the right time or the right place at the wrong time. Or both."

"Both?"

"You can even find your molecules get transmuted into another form."

"Seriously?"

John raised his eyebrows and nodded slightly. "Oh yeah. It 'appens. More often than you might like to think. One of the nipkows – I think it was nipkow2 – was apparently on 'is way to a conference on Omega Kasan. Never turned up. After a few days they figured out he'd been transmuted into a blanid, skulkin' around by the rocks out by the Mortian 'abitation pods."

I could do nothing but gape in horror.

I'm sure John noticed it. "Yeah," he continued. "Worm'ole travel is not the precise science you might think it is. The Mortians are loath to admit it, but as I understand it, the algorithms are subject to weird fluctuations. Casimir2 told me it's somethin' to do with the relationship between matter and antimatter during the moment of entry to a space-time conduit. I've no idea what that means really, but 'e mentioned things like oscillatin' sub-atomic particles and chaotic quantum stuff and spontaneous transformations. Mean anything to you?" I shook my head and he went on, "For the most part, the mechanisms are predictable, but sometimes they're about as stable as a 'ot air balloon in a tornado. And what's more, I don't think the Mortians can do anythin' about it when stuff goes wrong."

"Oh my god," I murmured, suddenly feeling Arctic-cold inside. "How often? I mean, is it possible to tell… Is there any way…"

"I s'pose," said John, "worm'ole accidents 'appen

about as often as you get plane crashes on Earth. That's what the Mortians tell me, anyway. An' people do it, because the rewards are like way greater than the risk of somethin' bad 'appenin'."

My most urgent priority had now changed. I desperately needed to persuade casimir2 to set up a comms link with Aysha. He had mentioned it before, hadn't he? But now I thought about it, how would Aysha know what to do? How could casimir2 contact her? She obviously didn't have one of those microwocky things. He was obviously lying. Again.

I was about to request another interview with the Mortians when I became aware of a disturbance just outside the door. Ollie had evidently trapped a pigeon in his net and the bird had decided it wasn't going to come quietly. Having escaped the net, it had half-flown, half-scrambled its way into the bar, dodging Ollie's grasping hands and flapping its wings frantically in an attempt to fly away. Hampered by an injured wing, it could only scuttle around in circles, until it reached the table where John and I were sitting. Ollie eventually got both his hands around it and finally brought the errant bird under his control.

"I'll wring its flamin' neck!" he threatened, evidently embarrassed by his botched capture attempt.

I can't really explain it, but there was something in that bird's eye as it looked up towards me – a look of animation and intelligence and… well, fury, I guess.

I placed a restraining hand on Ollie's arm. "No, don't kill it!" I said. "Please, don't kill it!" Taking the hapless pigeon from his hands, I carried it to the door, raised my arms and let it go. And it was like I was releasing something wonderful from the darkest depths of my soul. I can't explain it, but my heart was pounding, and I could feel the blood rushing through my veins.

MARCH OF THE PENGUINS

A meeting between me and casimir2 would have driven a wedge in the Mortian camp. It would have isolated polkingbeal67 and further damaged the consensus that was vital for a comprehensive solution to the nefeshchayan problem. Naturally, I guessed that that might be precisely what casimir2 would have wanted. So, I asked the nefeshchayans to set up a meeting between me, polkingbeal67 *and* casimir2. When I did so, it came as no surprise to me to be told that casimir2 had, in any event, insisted on being present at all interviews between me and polkingbeal67 or, indeed, *any* of the Mortians. For some unaccountable reason, yukawa3 also insisted on being present.

Casimir2 was hostile from the outset. When I challenged him about his proposed comms link with Aysha, he snarled, "She wouldn't be interested… wouldn't be interested anyway. If she cared about you, she wouldn't have gone back… gone back to Earth."

"As I understand it, she didn't get any choice," I countered. "Ollie told me what happened."

Casimir2 uttered a thin sound, a kind of whistle. "I

don't recall her putting up much of a fight," he said. "None of you erflings seem to care about one another. Surely, if any of them cared... cared about you, wouldn't they come looking for you?"

"I think they care..."

Casimir2 interrupted me. "You do? What do you suppose they've done? Put up a few posters?"

"They might not be looking for him," yukawa3 interjected, not very helpfully. "But I bet they're trying to find him."

"Well, you know perfectly well we haven't mastered wormhole travel on Earth. And nor, from what I've heard, have *you*. Not entirely, anyway. I've been talking to John and..."

"You are such primitive beings!" he snapped, interrupting me once again. "You are from an inferior race and you can never hope... never hope to overcome that inferiority."

"What? Just because we haven't mastered wormhole travel yet?" I asked defensively.

"You're not going to master it any time soon, either," said casimir2 disdainfully. "You've only had the ability to send any kind of transmissions... send transmissions out into space and travel away from your planet for a hundred years or so now.

And during that time you nearly extinguished yourselves with nuclear weapons. You almost self-destructed! You people don't even understand viability versing yet! You call it dark matter! It's as if you've barely discovered how to manipulate the momenta of the scalar particle."

"It's as if you don't think I'll pick you up and stuff you into the ice maker," I retorted, completely insulted, but oblivious to what he was talking about. "Anyway, some of your technology may have evolved faster than ours, but our planet is better looking than yours. Plus, we have paintballing weekends." Okay, I don't come up with the cleverest things on the spur of the moment.

"Don't make me laugh," casimir2 shook his head and smirked. "Have you even invented the wheel yet? Listen, don't worry. You'll be spending the rest of your days on a civilised planet - we'll do our best to help you catch up."

"And become totally obnoxious and insufferable?" I countered. "Well at least I'll be learning from the best. You're supremely arrogant, patronising and condescending. And you make it look so easy."

Yukawa3 offered a mollifying compliment, "There are definitely lower forms of life than earthling humans. Why, on Earth itself you've got creatures like scampi. Verily, we're all just at different points on the evolutionary scale. I constantly remind myself of something our revered leader, polkingbeal67, once told me. It's about a chillok living in a forest containing huge ancient trees. I've remembered almost the whole story, word for word."

Polkingbeal67 interrupted him. "I didn't tell you any such story."

He went on, completely oblivious to the leader's scowl. "So, the chillok's lifetime is so short that it never gets to see the birth or death of any of the trees. It looks around and sees some young saplings, perhaps nothing more than seeds just sprouting out of the ground. Then it sees average, middle-sized trees, and, of course, it sees the huge trees that form the canopy of the forest."

"That's not *my* story," polkingbeal67 insisted.

"It also sees some trees that have fallen and are decaying into the soil," yukawa3 continued. "So, in its entire lifetime, it sees all the stages of evolution of a tree, from seed to sapling to fully grown tree to dead trunks decomposing into the soil - the full cycle of evolution."

Like polkingbeal67, casimir2 looked distinctly unimpressed. "That's not a story at all. What's the point of it?" he asked.

"Yeah," said yukawa3, shrugging. "That's the bit I forgot. But what we must remember is that we're all human beings and we're all totally amazing creatures. Why, even an earthling, like Neil here, makes about thirty-five thousand conscious or semi-conscious decisions every single day!"

"What if they're all wrong?" sneered casimir2.

"Anyway, the thing is," yukawa3 continued doggedly, "earthling humans have totally perfected the sou'wester. Oh, and they've *definitely* invented the wheel. I don't know precisely who invented it, but I've been to Earth and, verily, I can vouch for it." Turning to me, he asked, "Who invented it?"

"Yes," said casimir2 sarcastically, knowing full well that we earthlings have no idea who invented the wheel. "He or she must be a very celebrated individual on your planet."

Perhaps yukawa3 noticed the exasperation in my eyes. "It's not important who invented the wheel," he said, apparently rushing to my defence. "It's the person who invented the other three wheels who should be celebrated."

As I remained indignantly silent, yukawa3 stood up, announcing that he would look it up on his microwocky and promptly left the table.

After a few snide utterances that weren't entirely audible, casimir2 cleared his throat and pointed at my head. "Your brains are far less evolved... far less evolved than ours. Our ancestors discovered your backward planet many eons ago. Who do you imagine built your pyramids and... and Stonehenge? Do the moai statues look like... look like *erfling* humans? I don't think so."

"My understanding is that you knew absolutely nothing about us until smolin9 and polkingbeal67 found the Voyager 1 space probe," I countered.

"Yes, well, we built Stonehenge and the other stuff straight after that. And... and who do you think killed all the dinosaurs... killed all the dinosaurs for you? Ex gratia."

A sour smile probably crossed my face despite my efforts to remain as composed and as uncombative as possible. "The dinosaurs disappeared about sixty-five million years ago at the end of the Cretaceous Period. The Voyager space probes were launched in 1977."

"Don't try to baffle me with, er, ... with history," said casimir2. "*Have* the dinosaurs disappeared or not? They don't trample you... don't trample you or chew off your heads any more, do they? You... you ingrates! You should... you should be grateful to us in perpetuum."

"You're a bit quiet," I said, turning to polkingbeal67.

"Sorry," he replied disinterestedly, fingering his eye patch. "I'm having trouble listening."

I knew I'd have my work cut out trying to keep the meeting on track before casimir2 derailed it completely, so I ignored all further crass attempts at provocation. "Let's get on," I said. "Here's my first question: can you assure me the nefeshchayans will all arrive safely on Earth?" And I couldn't resist adding, "Also, can you please assure me that Aysha got back okay."

"No," said polkingbeal67, absent-mindedly twiddling his furled umbrella.

"Yes," said casimir2.

"What?" I asked, looking uneasily from one to the other, "Which question are you answering?"

"Both," said casimir2.

"The first one," said polkingbeal67. "Oh, and the second one too." Having noticed my expression of utter confusion, he evidently thought it helpful to add, "Trust your intuition. The universe is guiding your life." With that, he repositioned a beer mat so that half of it protruded over the edge of the table. Flipping it up in the air with the back of his free hand, he attempted to hit it with a swish of the umbrella.

There was a pause for reflection or dumbfoundment or something, then I broached the matter of wormhole transit accidents. "I've heard from John that there have been some nasty mishaps. He told me about nipkow2 being transformed into a blanid on his way to a conference somewhere."

"We should not be criticised for that," casimir2 asserted.

"So, it's true?" I asked, shooting a look at polkingbeal67, who nodded.

Casimir2 simply shrugged, as if to say that it didn't matter.

"So, I can't give them any assurances concerning their safety?" I persisted.

"No," said polkingbeal67.

"Yes," casimir2 contradicted. "Nipkow2 was eventually restored… restored to his normal Mortian self."

"Oh," I asked. "How?"

"You won't understand," sneered casimir2. "Suffice to say, things are quite chaotic… chaotic at the quantum level, and sometimes energy threads interfere with the wormhole spec. In a successful wormhole transit, matter leaves a... leaves a kind of hole behind - antimatter, if you like. The protons leave negatively-charged anti-protons, electrons leave positively-charged anti-electrons and even the neutral particles leave anti-particles. It's a delicate and dynamic equilibrium that can easily... easily become upset by various external factors. Antimatter, you see, can be... can be rather unpredictable. But when mishaps occur, it's possible to reassemble the particles when you repeat... repeat the transit with modified parameters. It's all about unravelling the particle entanglement. But this is... this is way beyond the cognitive abilities of a mere erfling."

I tried not to appear too confounded, but I confess my brain had been thinking about pasta and antipasta the whole time he'd been speaking. Then my latent anxiety about Aysha bubbled once more to the surface. "Can you please confirm that Aysha got back to Earth in one piece?"

Neither of them would answer the question, no matter how much I persevered. Eventually, polkingbeal67 got to his feet, tapped his umbrella on the floor a couple of times, then leaned on it. "There's something else you should know," he said. "Let not this be whispered everywhere, but there's a reason why we don't want all the nefeshchayans to return to Earth."

A look of alarm crept across casimir2's face like a puddle of spilt ink. "This… this interview is terminated!" he declared with a flourish of his gnarled hand.

"Some of them are not of pure earthling extraction," continued polkingbeal67, apparently oblivious to casimir2's consternation.

"Terminated!" shrieked casimir2, rocking from foot to foot in extreme agitation, his eyes darting with rage. "This interview is terminated!"

"In my role as broker for peace," I told him, "I think *I*'ll decide when it's terminated. Now, what's this about some of the nefeshchayans not being earthlings?"

"Things are never quite the way they seem," said polkingbeal67. "I didn't say they weren't earthlings. I simply said they weren't *purely*…"

"Stop!" shrieked casimir2, leaping to his feet. "Entia non sunt multiplicanda praeter necessitate!"

At this point, everything happened very quickly. With a quick movement, casimir2 lunged for polkingbeal67's throat. Attempting to block him with my arm, I got knocked to the floor as a swing of the umbrella inadvertently caught me across the side of my head. Polkingbeal67's eyes opened wide with shock as casimir2's spindly arms encircled him. There was a moment when everything froze. Then yukawa3 appeared from nowhere, snatched the mutator from around casimir2's neck, threw a rug over his head and seized him with both arms.

As the other Mortians stood rooted in place, polkingbeal67 kicked over the table and stood behind it, alongside casimir2, who continued to kick and thrash around blindly as yukawa3 grappled with him. "It's the chilloks!" shouted polkingbeal67. "The chilloks have invaded his brain!"

"It's true," said yukawa3, struggling to subdue the captive's desperate efforts. "He's been compromised. We can't trust him. And if you think that's inconceivable, well, it is."

Having picked myself up off the floor, I tore off my shirt and, with polkingbeal67 and yukawa3's assistance, tied it around casimir2's writhing body. Restrained and secured to the table, casimir2 uttered a harrowing cry of fury and pain like a wolf on a deserted plain baying into the depths of the night. We finally had the mouse by the tail. Okay, maybe a wolf, maybe a mouse – I don't know, whatever - imagine a mouse that roars really loudly, or a wolf that has a pointed snout, small rounded ears and is kind of partial to cheese.

Anyway, the Mortians had a long and heated exchange in their native tongue. It became an argument, in which yukawa3 seemed to be making desperate appeals. Then polkingbeal67 tapped his umbrella insistently on the floor before abruptly hurrying towards a toilet door. Reluctantly at first, but then fully participating in the struggle, the Mortians bundled casimir2 through the toilet door and barricaded it using barrels and tables.

Okay," I said tentatively, breaking the silence. "So, this is possibly quite bad, isn't it? What do we do now?" Turning to polkingbeal67, I added, "Wait, first of all, I need to know what you meant when you said that some of the nefeshchayans are not pure earthlings."

In a rambling and occasionally incoherent manner, the leader explained to me that the threat of chillok takeover by insidious means had prompted the Mortians to experiment with a neuroscientific solution. He reasoned that if his people were to survive, they had to address the problem of 'happy' chemical deficiency. And the presence of earthlings, who, despite their 'hartglue' depletion, were blessed with perfectly tolerable levels of serotonin, dopamine, oxytocin and endorphins, offered an intriguing opportunity.

"What do you mean?" I asked.

"In order to safeguard the future of our species and yours, we've had to take certain measures. We've had to be on the lookout for future events which have cast their shadows beforehand."

"What it is," said yukawa3, nodding sagely like a carnival psychic. "What it is."

At this point, nipkow4 took it upon himself to deliver a long discourse on the subject of a Mortian attribute known as Karma 5. I've already made several references to the Mortian biomimetic mutator. Well, it seems that this phenomenal piece of kit not only facilitated metamorphosis into alternative life forms, but it also boasted a whole bunch of funky features that made it an absolutely essential facet of Mortian existence. It apparently stored a permanent copy of its owner's master configuration, so that it was always possible to default to his original physical Mortian form. It also preserved the quintessence or soul of its owner in automatically updateable codified form. This comprised all kinds of intangibles relating to the Mortian's personal essence - things such as his spirit, his character, his conscience and his personality - all the non-physical attributes that defined him.

According to nipkow4, a Mortian's Karma 5 was

theoretically a transferable entity. Although the practice of transferring someone's Karma 5 to another living entity had originally been proscribed by the Mortian authorities, exceptions had been granted in more recent times.

"You're telling me that some of the nefeshchayans have been given Mortian personalities?" I asked tentatively.

"Yes," said polkingbeal67 solemnly, jabbing the air with his umbrella. "Change can hurt, but it leads a path to something better."

I scratched my head, trying to figure it all out. "So, what happened to their original earthling personalities?"

It was a question that none of them seemed prepared to answer. Then nipkow4 replied, "They didn't have one."

"Didn't have a personality?" I asked quizzically, examining his face.

"Babies," he said. "We're talking about new-born infants here."

"How many?" I asked. "And how does it work? Which Mortians are sitting around here without their personalities?"

Nipkow4 made a high frequency whistling noise as he exhaled through his thin lips. And I think he may have rolled his eyes. "Two," he said. "And they still have their personalities. Typically, the Karma 5 copy is stored on our mutators. In the case of these two individuals, the copies have been transferred to the nefeshchayan babies. And the Karma 5 contains hartglue."

I was beginning to grasp the full implications of all this. So, in order to thwart the chilloks, the Mortians had engineered an interspecific hybrid capable of generating exactly the kind of cocktail of neurotransmitters required to render the cerebrum ambulans ineffective and harmless. "Well," I said, as I gathered my thoughts. "How would you know if it works? And why just two people? And who are they?"

"Do you mean who are the two nefeshchayans?" asked nipkow4. "Or who are the two Mortians?"

"Er, both?" I responded, shrugging.

"Keep your eye out for special people," said yukawa3 with an air of pompous dignity.

Nipkow4 fixed me with an earnest gaze. "The nefeshchayans are, like I said, two new-born babies. As for the Mortians, they are smolin10 and the unnamed one."

"The unnamed one?"

"That's me," said a mysterious voice from somewhere at the back of the group of onlookers. Craning his neck to get our attention, he opened his mouth to say more and then drew back in timidity.

"Why do you call him the unnamed one?" I asked nipkow4.

"Because he has no name," he replied, a little tersely. "He is the next generation of our former leader, who we referred to as 'our revered leader'. He had no name as such. And now, we have a new revered leader…"

"Hmm, yes, I can see how it might have got confusing if you'd given his clone the same moniker," I said. Indeed, there *was* some logic there somewhere, but it was the kind of logic that got you from A to B when you wanted to be at C. "And smolin10 is the next generation of smolin9?"

"That's right. As I'm sure you know, the planet was formerly named after him." Nipkow4 was drumming his slender fingers impatiently on the table. "We've restricted the experiment to just two test cases at present. We know the chemical balance works in terms of warding off cerebrum ambulans, but there's been no evaluation of the risk factors for side effects. And that's why the experimental group is small at present."

"And that's also why you can't send all the nefeshchayans to Earth," I mused. "Well, what have you learned so far?"

"We've observed that on days when one of the trial subjects cries during the night, a cloud crosses in front of one of our moons. Also, there is a greater likelihood of a dispute about food distribution amongst the nefeshchayans. We believe there's a connection."

Shaking my head as if that would make all this nonsense go away, I mumbled some comment about correlation not implying causation, but nipkow4 was undeterred. His voice dropped an octave and concern was etched on his face as he spoke: "The babies are not in touch with their own humanity and therefore fail to see humanity in others. Indeed, we've observed that they consider others to represent a threat to their power and influence. It could be that they've been taken over by a psychosis that eats away at other people's psychic energies. They consume without giving anything back, continually draining and impoverishing the resources of the community."

My eyes could not have opened any wider. Apart from anything else, the Mortians clearly had no concept of child development. And I told them so.

After confronting them with their hopeless misreading of the situation, I concluded by asking them how many nefeshchayans would be permitted to leave for Earth. What would it be? All of them, none of them or just a few selected individuals? And then it crossed my mind that they might intend to copy all their Karma 5 configurations to earthling hosts.

"Oh no! Definitely not!" Nipkow4 was emphatic. "You're totally on the wrong track. Earthling bodies have such a meagre shelf-life! We couldn't possibly consider such a preposterous solution."

So, they were evidently contemplating the possibility of making switches in the *other* direction – transferring earthling neurotransmitter metabolism to Mortian hosts. "Have you worked out how to do it?" I asked.

Nipkow4 tilted his head and looked sideways at me. "How to do what?"

"How to import our 'happy' chemicals into your Karma 5 configurations?"

"It's not about us," nipkow4 told me with all the sincerity of a hungry wolf reassuring a trapped lamb. "It's about doing what's best for the babies."

I now felt as uncomfortable with nipkow4 as I did

with casimir2. Was it possible that this most obsequious and punctilious of Mortians was *also* being manipulated by the notorious chillok brain tuners?

Polkingbeal67 poked my arm to get my attention. "Happiness is not just chemicals," he whispered, twirling the umbrella before opening it with a snap.

"No," I conceded. "That's right. It's not. And music is not just vibrations. But sometimes it *does* help to pare these concepts down to their most basic elements, if only because we all need analytical chemistry solutions to rid us of the chillok problem."

Polkingbeal67 peered out from under his umbrella. "I wish to return to my home, the palace of obsidian fingers," he announced with an air of solemnity and significance.

"Yeah, there's no place like home," I said, feeling like I was suddenly in Wizard of Oz territory. "We *all* want to get back home. You should be glad that at least that's possible for you. It's not possible for me."

Polkingbeal67 put down his umbrella and wrapped a frond of seaweed around his arm. "Something you lost will soon turn up," he said.

"Knowing my luck it'll be the stone and a half I lost after last Christmas," I replied.

Struggling to ascertain the motives of all the parties involved in the predicament I found myself in, I decided to focus on the most unfathomable of all of them – I needed to figure out the rationale behind the chilloks' strategy. "If sound strategy starts with having the right goal, how would you define the chilloks' objectives?" I asked no one in particular.

No one in particular answered, so I rephrased it: "What are the chilloks playing at?"

"Let me think about it," said yukawa3. Sometimes the brain can receive too much information, sometimes not enough. With yukawa3, it didn't seem to make any difference. "I give up," he added almost instantly.

Polkingbeal67, still engaged in wrapping his arm in seaweed, apparently felt compelled to say: "A strategy without any tactics is a slow, slow route to victory."

"Are you saying they know what they want but don't know how to go about achieving it?" I asked. I soon wished I hadn't.

"I have the answer to that one!" yukawa3 interjected urgently. Unfortunately, he didn't.

"Their tactics seem clear enough," I said. "Seems to me they're manipulating casimir2 to do two things. One is to cause division and dissent among yourselves and the other is to control immigration and emigration between here and Earth."

Polkingbeal67 tugged at the rubbery, tubular-shaped piece of seaweed and responded, "Tactics without a strategy is just noise before a defeat."

It was nipkow4 who eventually injected a modicum of rationality into the discussion. "The chilloks would want to sever any connection between our planet and yours," he said.

"Makes sense," I nodded. That seemed to me to be a perfectly reasonable theory. If the full range of 'happy' chemicals could only be achieved by some sort of synthesis between our two humanoid species, it followed that the chilloks would want the nefeshchayans (and me) evicted from Melinda and future travel between the planets forestalled in some way. And, clearly, of course, it implied that they were prepared to kill me to achieve that end. It was a sobering thought, certainly, but one that was wrenched from my mind by the urgency of all the other problems I had to solve. Would it be prudent to disable the wormhole portal? Or would that simply risk alienating and antagonising the nefeshchayans? There was also the pressing issue of what to do about casimir2. For as long as he remained under the influence of the chilloks (and locked in the toilet), there was no prospect of any of the nefeshchayans returning to their ancestral homeland.

Having decided my priority had to be to get the Mortians and the nefeshchayans singing from the same hymn sheet, I focused on the conceivability of John being able to talk things through sensibly with one of the Mortians. But, given that polkingbeal67 was incoherent and rather unhinged, and nipkow4 had no express or implied authority, this was not going to be easy. As the Mortians were effectively rudderless, I considered convening an open meeting of *all* the nefeshchayans and *all* the Mortians. If I'm honest, however, I thought this would be at best pointless and at worst a catastrophe.

I still believed there was something to be gained from my role as an intermediary, so while the Mortians bickered and quarrelled in their native tongue, I sat back and reflected on the Robbers Cave Experiment, a famous study investigating group conflict dating back to the last century. It purported to show how people who were loath to cooperate for a positive cause were motivated to unite and rally against a common enemy.

Unclear as to how to proceed, I summoned all my

powers of oratory, fluffed my lines, tripped over my tongue and made a real mess of things. One thing was becoming abundantly clear: this was becoming a very difficult and a very fraught situation and my role as a go-between was proving to be beyond me. Then suddenly, a fortuitous event occurred. Alerted by a sudden frenetic flurry of wings, we all spotted a pigeon that had apparently flown through the skylight and had now found a comfortable vantage point on a beam, cooing melodiously. After a few seconds, it flew down onto the table in the corner, fluttered its feathers in agitation and started clawing and pecking at casimir2's mutator. Taking off again with a frantic beating of wings, it completed a couple of circuits of the ceiling above our heads and disappeared once more through the skylight.

Turning to nipkow4, I felt compelled to remark, "If you people can disguise yourselves using your mutator things, why haven't you tried changing into something small, and escaping from here?"

"The biomimetic mutator is designed principally for *humanoid* disguises," said nipkow4 with a supercilious air and the dismissive wave of the hand he always used when anyone said anything he deemed unworthy of serious attention.

"But not *exclusively* humanoid?" I persisted. "We've all seen yukawa3 transformed into a penguin."

The Mortians looked at one another in an apparent state of bewilderment and, for reasons that defy easy explanation, I waddled across the floor backwards - for some sort of dramatic effect, I suppose. I knocked on the door, and the nefeshchayan on guard duty let me out.

. . .

The debriefing had barely started when the same guard rushed in with a look of panic and consternation on his face. "It's not my fault!" he insisted. "There was this pitiful growlin' noise like a sand-clogged 'overcruiser failin' to start. To be 'onest, I thought they 'actually 'ad an 'overcruiser in there. So, yeah, I opened the door and they rushed me!"

John whirled on his heels and ran to the door. "What? You idiot! You let the Mortians escape?"

The sight that met our eyes as we followed him into the corridor was so extraordinary that we could scarcely believe the evidence of our own senses. At the far end of the corridor were a couple of dozen emperor penguins, marching in single file like a regiment of poorly drilled, poorly disciplined, diminutive black-and-white draftees. Jostling and bumping into each other, they croaked like frogs, honked like geese and brayed like donkeys. The one at the back of the parade stopped, bent forward, lifted his tail and, with remarkable gastrointestinal force, projectile-pooped profusely onto the polished floor. With a quick and ungainly scamper, he rejoined the troop and, one by one, they tottered and shuffled out of the door leading to the yard.

DISCLOSURE

Penguins are surprisingly hard to catch. Not only are their bodies slippery with oil, but also, they're quick, agile, startlingly strong and they lash out with their long, hooked beaks. The hapless nefeshchayans made a total and utter spectacle of themselves trying to capture the animated, feathery fugitives as they cavorted around in comical, wobbly disarray. But what made it one of the best days of my life was the moment when a small herd of guanacos suddenly appeared around the far corner of the compound. The llama-like guanacos were scared and skittish to begin with, adopting submissive crouches by lowering their necks, bending their knees and raising their tails. But they grew in confidence, and before long their tails were wagging like flags in a hurricane, and they started chasing the penguins, kicking, spitting and making a hideous din with their high trills and guttural clicking noises.

But, entertaining as it was to witness the pandemonium, I had to contemplate my next move.

I must admit that selfish concerns were beginning to cloud my judgement. I simply didn't think I was capable of adopting a purely objective and altruistic approach any longer. When you face death or permanent exile, I guess you have to readjust your priorities. To be frank, I didn't relish the idea of seeing out my days on this planet without the comforting benefits and behaviours of earthling society. So, almost without knowing it, I had become predisposed to opposing the nefeshchayans' aspirations.

One of the nefeshchayans shot me a baleful look and walked past me, clutching the side of his face with a bloodied handkerchief. He was muttering and swearing in anguish. Apparently, getting stabbed in the cheek with a penguin bill is not as funny as it may sound.

Obviously, the chilloks posed an incredibly serious and existential threat to humanity generally and to both of our civilisations, Earthling and Mortian, in particular. The common threat had created a mutual dependency. I could therefore make a case for some of the nefeshchayans remaining on Melinda. But that raised all kinds of questions. For one thing, I couldn't imagine how I might break the news to the parents of the hybrid babies.

Meanwhile, Lizzie rushed past with one of the penguins clasped beneath one arm, while she clamped the beak shut in her other hand. "Life is just a bowl of cherries," she said, rolling her eyes sarcastically. "What exactly *are* cherries?" she asked over her shoulder as she disappeared inside.

The thought of cherries only served to fuel my anxiety. My dad had been a keen gardener and had told me about the variety of symbiotic relationships ants have developed not only with other invertebrates but also with plants like the cherry tree. He told me, for example, that ants have developed an intriguing partnership with aphids that feed on the cherry tree sap. The ants stimulate the aphids to release a waste product known as honeydew, a liquid that provides them with energy and nutrients. For their part, the aphids benefit because the ants attack their sapsucking competitors. And that's not all. The cherry trees themselves benefit because the ants fiercely attack caterpillars and other leaf-eating bugs that target the soft, tender new leaves for nourishment during springtime. In return, the tree rewards its guardians with sweet nectar produced from nectaries, small red lumps at the base of the new leaves. This just demonstrates how sneaky, devious and sinister all these ant-related creatures really are.

The more I thought about it, the more I figured I had cause to worry. If the only protection against chillok infiltration was a balance of 'happy' chemicals, including hartglue, what were the long-term prospects for humans on Earth? As I understood it from talking to yukawa3, biologists on Earth were a very long way away from having the capacity to replicate an endogenous chemical like hartglue. In fact, our biologists had not even *discovered* hartglue yet.

So, assuming a successful migration of nefeshchayans to Earth could be achieved and assuming they took as many vials of hartglue as they could carry, the vaccines derived from it would only have limited distribution and could not be replicated and therefore would not protect future generations. The only way to insure future generations of earthling humans against the risk of chillok infiltration was by altering the genetic coding. I was beginning to realise that this meant that at least one of the hybrid babies would have to be sent to Earth. And even that represented the most tenuous and fragile prospect imaginable.

Meanwhile, one by one, the penguins were noisily and unceremoniously rounded up and returned to confinement in the Irish bar, the one with the golf mural, where they were reunited with their mutators.

I went inside and found ten recaptured penguins milling about like travellers stranded at an airport, along with three Mortians – yukawa3, the unnamed one and another, who I assumed was smolin10.

I looked at yukawa3. "You didn't want to transform yourself into a penguin, then?"

He shook his head.

"What about you two?" I asked, turning to the unnamed one and smolin10.

Yukawa3 took me aside and answered for them. "Their mutators aren't functional without the Karma 5 copies."

"But they'll work okay when you've, y'know, completed the hybrid experiment?"

Yukawa3 looked at me askance as if I'd suggested something egregiously terrible. "Verily, I need to speak to you privately," he said.

We sat in a corner where no one could overhear us and yukawa3 leaned across and whispered conspiratorially, "If anyone asks you what I'm about to tell you, you don't know."

"Don't know what?" I asked. "What are you going to tell me?"

"I can't tell you that."

"Well, who's going to ask me?" I asked, shrugging in confusion.

"No, I can't tell you that either."

"You're asking me not to tell anyone something you can't tell me?"

Yukawa3 nodded with an earnest look.

"And you can't tell me who might ask?"

"Let me think about this," he said.

"Yeah, you really need to think this through."

After a short pause, during which he stared vacantly at the table, he nodded again. "Okay, I've thought it through."

"Okay," I said. "So, if someone, anyone - and we don't know who this might be… if they ask me what you said, what should I say?"

"I don't know. Tell them I told you about the intergalactic zoo on Omega Kasan."

I don't really know why I asked this, but I did. "*Is* there a zoo on Omega Kasan?"

"No."

"Well, what if they were to ask me a follow up question?" I queried. "Like something about the animals."

"Just say I told you about the zoo and you don't remember anything else."

"Okay," I agreed in exasperation.

A few of the penguins started peeping shrilly. They were struggling to operate their mutators. As yukawa3 disappeared to the other side of the bar to attend to them, the unnamed one and smolin10 were stealing furtive glances at me out of the corners of their eyes. Eventually, smolin10 sidled up to me and said, "You were asking why we didn't do the penguin thing."

"Yes," I nodded.

"There was no point, was there?" he said with a strange gesture of his hands that was probably intended to indicate how one must put up with all manner of idiotic ideas. But it looked more like a pair of bats dancing at dusk. "Why did they think they'd be able to escape like that?"

"Yeah," I shrugged. "Penguins can't fly."

"But that's not the only reason we didn't join in."

"I know."

"What did he tell you?" The unnamed one asked, joining in the conversation.

"Yukawa3? Er, nothing," I said, mindful of yukawa3's watchful gaze from the other side of the bar. "He was telling me about the zoo."

"He must think we're idiots," said smolin10. "None of them are prepared to tell us the truth. About our mutators."

"The truth?" I asked. "So, yeah, they're, uh, temporarily out of action because of the babies and the Karma 5 experiment thing?"

Smolin10 repeated the strange gesture with his hands. "They think we don't know this, but… it's not temporary." His face wore an expression of sheer abhorrence. Clearly, this was a very big deal to them.

"Not temporary," I echoed pointlessly.

"No," the unnamed one confirmed. "Their secret is out. Never carry grain in a bag with a hole. Anyway, while they're all still busy being penguins, you might like to know something we've discovered. You see, *we* know something *they* don't know."

"You do?"

"We've been monitoring things on our microwockys," explained smolin10. "And we've noticed something. Something important."

They fell quiet, so I felt obliged to prompt them. "What is it?" I asked. "What have you been monitoring?"

With a sharp intake of breath, smolin10 shook his head slowly, pursed his lips and said, "We monitor all kinds of stuff. Like the concentration of oxygen in the atmosphere. Do you earthlings know anything about oxygen?"

I was both amused and taken aback by this. "Of course," I said. "We're not *that* primitive, y'know! We discovered oxygen way back. I think it was a guy called Priestley and it was at the end of the eighteenth century."

Smolin10 cast me a sidelong glance. "So, what did you people breathe before that?"

"No, I…I don't mean… Oh, for Pete's sake!" I replied with irritation. "Well, *is* it to do with oxygen?"

Smolin10 shook his head. "No, it's nothing to do with oxygen," he said. "It's to do with the chilloks. Our microwockys can detect the presence of cerebrum ambulans within a radius of five of your earthling kilometres."

"I know," I nodded in encouragement.

Another frenzied whirl of his hands and then he told

me something that truly took my breath away (and it wasn't related to the monitoring of oxygen): "Thing is, now we can't detect any."

Was he saying what I thought he was saying? "Your microwockys are broken?" I asked, seeking clarification.

"The words 'listen' and 'silent' use the same letters," said the unnamed one, cryptically and critically. "We can't detect them because they've gone. The cerebra ambulans have left the building."

"Oh, I see," I said, slapping my hand to my forehead. "You mean casimir2. So, casimir2 is no longer being manipulated by the chilloks?"

They both nodded with enthusiasm.

SOME DAYS YOU'RE THE PIGEON...

Polkingbeal67 blamed me for the penguin escape fiasco. "The tongue can paint what the eye can't see. And you painted penguins with your words," he insisted. "You suggested we should transform ourselves into penguins."

"I did no such thing," I objected. "I simply reminded you that you could assume other life forms. Other than humanoid, that is. By the way, you are now in a position to negotiate with the nefeshchayans with all options on the table."

"How is that possible?" polkingbeal67 asked. "We cannot offer them wormhole transit as casimir2 is controlled by the chilloks. And he must remain under lock and key."

"Well, there's the thing," I said. "You and smolin10 and the unnamed one need to have an open and honest conversation right now."

I beckoned them over and left them to it. Trained singers on Earth don't typically exceed a two-to-four-octave range and most of us manage to express the whole gamut of emotion and complexity of mood within just two octaves. It would appear that Mortian voices are more attuned to their emotional impulses. When they get excited, they are capable of many more octaves than us. I sat and marvelled at the passion and despair in their voices as the cacophony ebbed and flowed and eventually receded to an exhausted whimpering.

Afterwards, polkingbeal67 wandered slowly over to me. He resembled a slender stem of tall grass buffeted by the wind. Well, except for the slender bit. "It is late," he said wearily. "We all need rest. The night will rinse what the day has soaped."

"But first we must release casimir2," I told him.

"*Must* we?" His eyes drooped in a most pathetic way. "A cornered dog will leap over a wall."

"He'll be different now," I assured him. "His brain is no longer contaminated. He won't be looking to overthrow you or anything like that."

His scowl took on a baleful quality. "Perhaps the enemy of my enemy is my friend," he mumbled cryptically. "If someone betrays you once, it's *his* fault. If he betrays you twice, it's *your* fault. And, in this case, I do mean *your* fault." He fixed me with a stare he no doubt intended to penetrate the very core of my being.

"We must trust him now," I contended. "It's the key to everything."

"Are you sure?" he asked. "Perhaps, in view of his treacherous behaviour, we should insist that he donate his body to science with immediate effect. And then maybe we should slice his brain really thin like a joint of your earthling bacon to verify that the cerebra ambulans have really gone."

"Come on," I urged him. "Honey is better than sour grapes. You've got an opportunity to demonstrate some real leadership qualities here. Your people need that now."

He ducked behind the bar for a couple of minutes, then reappeared, festooned with a garland of seaweed. With no small amount of pomp, he opened the umbrella, held it over his head and delivered a booming rendition of what I assume was some kind of rousing Mortian anthem.

Yukawa3 clasped his hands together as if to pray, closed his eyes and mumbled, "It is spoken." Whereupon all the Mortians arose with one accord, hastened to the nearest wall and gently beat their heads against it.

Once this bizarre ceremony was completed, polkingbeal67 and nipkow4 released casimir2 from his confinement in the toilet.

With all the reserve of a panhandler discovering gold, yukawa3 rushed over and took hold of casimir2's arm. "He's got a pulse!" he declared, grinning from ear to ear (well, I'm sure that might have applied if he'd possessed external ears). Perplexed, he added, "Wait, no, that's *my* pulse."

Casimir2 shook him off and stepped forward, looking genuinely contrite and distressed. "I don't really know what I did," he said. "But it must have been terrible to warrant you locking me up like that."

"You've not been yourself," said polkingbeal67.

"I just don't know what happened," said casimir2, a distraught expression in his eyes. "I felt a strange... strange pain in my head."

"What did it feel like?" asked nipkow4, evidently taking a keen interest in casimir2's experience. I was aware that he was keen to document all incidents of chillok incursion. "Was it a familiar sensation? Was it like something you've had before?"

"Now you mention it, yes, I think so," he replied.

"Well, you've had it again," said yukawa3, nodding judiciously.

Casimir2 turned to nipkow4. "Was it the chilloks?"

Nipkow4 put a reassuring arm around his shoulders. "Yes, we believe so. But it's okay, they're gone now."

Still distraught, casimir2 whimpered, "I'm a failure. A total failure. I should have been able to resist them. I feel like... like I let everyone down."

"It wasn't your fault," said nipkow4. "It could have happened to any of us. You're not a failure. Come on, that's just negative thinking."

"No," said casimir2, wretchedly. "I'm positive... positive I'm a failure. But do you know what the worst thing is? It's my memory. I can't recall anything that happened."

"Forget about it," suggested yukawa3 helpfully.

"Well, at least it's all over now," said smolin10. "How do you feel?"

"How do I feel?" echoed casimir2, slumping into his seat next to nipkow4. "I've had my brain invaded... invaded by creatures related to ants, I've been stranded in the desert with nothing but an erfling for company, I've been headbutted... headbutted by the planetary leader, I've had a jug of methane water thrown over me and I've been locked for hours in a... in a toilet. How do you *think* I feel?"

Smarting at the derogatory reference to myself, I was tempted to tell him he was certainly looking flushed, but I resisted it. Instead, I asked if any of them had a theory as to why the cerebra ambulans had abandoned their host.

"It's okay," said casimir2. "I don't have any abandonment issues."

Astonished, I stared and stared at him, trying to read the facial cues, but his mouth hung open and his expression was devoid of any signs of intentional humour.

The general consensus was that the cerebra ambulans had been deterred by the realisation that earthling-Mortian hybrids were already present in the population, undermining the chilloks' plans for world domination.

"And that's how I saved the world!" announced smolin10.

"And me," re-joined the unnamed one.

"Yes, I guess you did," I smiled at them. "And without either of you wearing a red cape! But, tell me this, what are the chances of the chilloks coming back?"

The Mortians looked at one another in a state of bewilderment. Yukawa3 cleared his throat. "Do you mean in terms of mathematical probability?" he asked.

"Er, yeah, okay, whatever," I replied. "Will they come back?"

"They might do," he declared with as much authority as he could muster. "It's fifty-fifty."

"That's ridiculous," scoffed casimir2. "It's not fifty-fifty."

"Yes, verily, it is," insisted yukawa3. "Either they come back… or they don't. Fifty-fifty."

"Yeah," I said, "I don't think that's how probability works."

Notwithstanding the anxiety and uncertainty posed by the chilloks, I now believed I could bring the nefeshchayans and the Mortians together for meaningful negotiations. Everything was coming together, and casimir2 seemed amenable, so I sat with polkingbeal67 and nipkow4 and drew up an agenda for talks.

"What arbitration expertise do you actually have?" asked nipkow4 as I was about to leave the bar to summon the nefeshchayans.

Put like that, I don't suppose I had any such experience at all. "Well, none, really," I admitted.

"Except that…" I left the sentence hanging - the only conflicts I had ever resolved involved playing rock-paper-scissors.

Turning on my heels, I repeated my question about Aysha. It had been eating me up inside and, even though I'd been slightly reluctant to face it head-on, I couldn't drop it either: had she or had she not been safely transported to Earth?

Casimir2 looked about as comfortable as a pig in an abattoir. "I fear not," he said.

"What do you mean? How so?" I demanded.

Casimir2 started pacing back and forth. For some reason, yukawa3 joined him. Polkingbeal67 spoke softly, "Please, can we leave it at that?"

I shook my head. "Nope," I said. "No, definitely not. Tell me what the hell has happened. Tell me now!"

"Accidents spring from the deepest source of destiny," said polkingbeal67. "There was a mishap. We believe she was transmuted into another life-form."

I must have been chewing my bottom lip so hard, I could taste blood. "What *kind* of life-form?" I asked as calmly as I could.

"Oh, um, a pigeon," polkingbeal67 mumbled nonchalantly.

"A pigeon!" I exclaimed. "What? No way! You can't possibly be serious! It's insane. I mean, is that even possible?"

"Do you mean in terms of mathematical probability?" asked yukawa3, who certainly deserved the withering look I directed at him. I was daring him to say it had been a fifty-fifty chance.

Actually, a few things now started to make sense. No, who was I kidding? *None* of this made any sense. "Which one?" I asked, as my brain proceeded to go numb.

"Which one?" polkingbeal67 repeated in little more than a whisper.

I gestured helplessly with my arms and appealed to casimir2. "Come on, help me out here. Which pigeon? Do you know which one is Aysha? Have you tried the repeat process thing you told me about?"

After a silence that spoke for itself, casimir2 started pacing around again. "It could have been worse," he said.

"Excuse me," I said. "My friend has been turned into what my mother used to describe as a 'rat with wings!' She does nothing but bob her head, peck at stuff and poop on people's heads. On top of that, you don't even know which one she is! And you say it could have been worse?"

I may have imagined it, but I swear there was a collective gulp.

"Pigeons aren't so bad," ventured casimir2, still pacing in circles. "According to the extensive research I've carried out, they adapt… they adapt to a wide variety of different habitats and they fully integrate… integrate into human environments."

I said nothing, but simply locked my eyes on him.

He continued, "And that's an intelligent trait that ensures… ensures their survival, way beyond the time other avian species become extinct."

By this time, I think my body had gone into shock. I was shaking like a leaf with agitation, and I was rocking as if I was on a boat.

Still, casimir2 went on, "Pigeons played a significant role… a significant role in one of your world wars. They made a real impact, carrying messages that provided intelligence to and fro… to and fro between various military units and resistance networks."

Finally, I found my voice and managed to stammer

out a somewhat weak, "Uh, really? Now listen to me, you little… Just listen to me! What are you going to do about it? How can we bring her back? There must be a solution to this. Come on, what's the answer?"

"We may not find an answer," polkingbeal67 intoned quietly. "A bird does not sing because it has an answer. It sings because it has a song. We must endeavour to listen and enjoy the song."

It was all I could do to keep myself from strangling him. It also now occurred to me that when casimir2 had been under the malevolent control of the chilloks, he had lied to me by offering to set up a wormhole communication channel so that I could speak to Aysha on Earth.

So, Aysha was still on this planet, albeit in the guise of a stout-bodied, short-necked, red-legged bird with greenish-purple iridescence around her feathers and a wingspan of about seventy centimetres. But it was Aysha. So, if I went outside in the yard and she was there, waddling about, pecking for food, and she turned around and our eyes met, what were we supposed to do? Should we race towards one another like two souls long separated by cruel fate, one tearing along at five miles an hour with arms outstretched, the other cooing and hopping valiantly with wings flapping wildly to keep her balance? For a moment or two I teetered on that precariously fragile line between laughter and torment. Then I fell splat on the less agreeable side.

Eventually, after what seemed an eternity of pain and despair, I hauled myself to my feet and crossed to the door.

.   .   .

You know that feeling when you think "This couldn't possibly get any worse", but then it just does? I walked disconsolately from the Irish bar where the Mortians were being held to a kitchen area where a few of the nefeshchayans were chatting and relaxing. Still stunned and weakened by my inability to process what had happened to Aysha, I was only vaguely aware of the woman with the skull tattoo on her cheek sitting over a bucket, a grubby cloth spread over her legs. Before my brain had fully registered what was happening, she had cut off the head of a pigeon at the base of the neck with a pair of scissors, and was about to start plucking the feathers.

"No!' I yelled. "No, no, no! What are you doing?"

"I'm getting the dinner ready," she replied. "Why?"

I gasped. My heart pounded, my voice trembled,

and my hand flew over my mouth. I could feel the blood draining from my face.

Noticing my distress, the woman with the skull tattoo put the bird down and offered me a cup of coffee. "Sorry if the sight of it upsets you," she said as soothingly as she could. "Ollie brought it in earlier. It's the first one he's caught."

"You've cut off her head!" I growled in a primal howl of rage that surprised even me. "How can we restore her now?"

"Restore 'er? 'Ow d'ya mean?" The woman placed the feathery corpse in her palm and thoroughly inspected it, lifting one wing and then the other. "Okay, the 'ead's obviously missin' now, but the rest of it's just fine," she declared.

WE ARE FAMILY

There wasn't an indoor room big enough to hold everybody, but it was certainly warm enough to sit outside in the yard. Melinda's eccentric orbit of its two suns gave rise to fairly extreme climate variations and this was a hot season. There was an ominous stillness in the air and I thought I discerned a muted rumble of thunder in the distance. In order to convey a sense of equality and balance, I had wanted everyone to gather in a large circle for the meeting, but John insisted that two concentric circles should be formed, the Mortians being on the inside facing the nefeshchayans in the outer circle. As a concession, polkingbeal67 was permitted to sit in the outer circle between me and John.

The Mortian leader delayed his arrival until the last possible moment and made a grand entrance, fingering his crystal necklace with one hand, brandishing his umbrella with the other, while two Mortians escorted him, gripping one arm each. The pair proudly hung onto him as if he were a prize exhibit at a county fair. Of course, he didn't actually *need* any assistance, but I suppose it was some kind of symbolic gesture of reverence, and it imparted a sense of occasion to the proceedings. The nefeshchayan children were restless and unsettled. One of the babies cried and had to be comforted. It felt like hours before everyone was seated. Then it was finally time for me to get the ball rolling.

Just as I stood up and opened my mouth to speak, yukawa3, seated directly opposite me, reached across and whispered urgently, "This is a momentous historic event, is it not? Verily, we'll all be participating in a meeting that will possibly have far-reaching consequences for both our planets. Do you not agree?"

"Yeah, I guess so," I nodded slowly. I was still reeling from the shock of seeing the headless pigeon, but I'd been trying to take comfort from the law of averages – I'd seen a flock of several dozen pigeons earlier in the day. There was no overwhelming reason to suppose Aysha had been beheaded. Besides, for now, I had to focus on resolving the conflict between the Mortians and the nefeshchayans, especially since the prospects for wormhole travel were now looking so much more encouraging.

"May we be permitted to fly our flag?" yukawa3 asked, producing a singularly unimpressive piece of fabric, embroidered with squiggly elliptical arcs composed of overlapping circles.

"What the…?" I bit my tongue before continuing. "So, is that your flag?"

"You like it?" His eyes lit up. "Let me tell you the story behind it."

"What now?" A few people were starting to get fidgety.

Yukawa3 clasped his knees with his hands. "Verily, in the beginning of life on the planet, methane clouds were inclined to spontaneously auto-ignite. The ancient Mortians believed these phenomena were the work of the goddess Theta Flying Pigs…"

I tried to interrupt him, but it was too late. He was in full flow:

"…who was said to be angry with the Great Orbis Bird who insisted on constantly interrupting her with his demands for more rain."

John coughed to get my attention, and polkingbeal67 tapped his umbrella impatiently. Yukawa3 continued regardless, "The incessant praying didn't cease, so she eventually felt compelled to pick him up and throw him to the fish in her celestial pond in the heavens. Legend has it that he ricocheted off the head of a water deity known as Gaff Tor and bounced between planet and heavens until he landed in the nefeshchaya lake and drowned. I hope that answers your question."

"Okay, so what do all those circular squiggles

represent exactly?" I asked.

"The bouncing between planet and heavens."

"Uh? The bouncing?"

"The bouncing," he confirmed.

Having attached the flag to a telescopic pole, he started waving it over his head to the annoyance of the Mortians on the far side of the circle who had turned their chairs around to face John and polkingbeal67. "It's upside down!" someone shouted.

As yukawa3 lowered the flag to check the orientation, casimir2 snatched it from him. "Fine," said yukawa3, pouting. "If you insist on unleashing the wrath of the gods…"

Right on cue, a prodigious burst of lightning ignited the methane-rich air to produce a whirling yellow and blue ball of fire. Dramatically reflected on the surface of the nefeshchayan lake, the phenomenon lasted plenty long enough for yukawa3 to wallow in smug satisfaction. "If that seems portentous, well, it is," he proclaimed, theatrically. But even *he* jumped on hearing the earth-shattering clap of thunder that followed.

Everyone finally settled down. After I proposed a vague agenda and nipkow4 delivered some preliminary remarks relating to the chilloks, polkingbeal67 adjusted his battered sherg-encrusted helmet, took to his feet, leaned on the umbrella to steady himself and collapsed in a heap as the umbrella inexplicably snapped.

Defiantly maintaining his composure and dignity, he rose, replaced his helmet, tossed both parts of the umbrella across the yard and addressed the gathered crowd in a voice at once warm and authoritative. "I greet you in a spirit of repentance and peace and humility. We have always been overwhelmed by our incompatibility. Furthermore, we are all guilty of making no effort to respect our differences. But we have a common enemy, and we now depend on each other for the survival of both our species. When the nest is overturned, no egg remains unbroken."

There was a brief interruption as another flash of lightning spooked the children. "It is spoken," said yukawa3, bowing obsequiously.

Polkingbeal67 went on, "Before I continue, please listen to the words of my learned friend, nipkow4, who will reveal to you some developments of which you are not aware – developments that will possibly upset you."

Nipkow4 rose slowly to his feet to speak to a hushed audience. His long-winded, repetitious and often tedious explanation of 'happy' chemical deficiency and hartglue depletion irritated everyone to the point where polkingbeal67 unwound a length of seaweed from around his neck and snapped it to express his displeasure. Nipkow4's subsequent clarification of the transfer of Karma 5 to two nefeshchayan babies was brief and rather vague. Nevertheless, it was met with gasps of astonishment and disbelief.

Polkingbeal67 stood up, clasped his hands and waited for hush. "Trees do not seek liberation from the soil, but, nevertheless, we uprooted you. We don't expect your forgiveness and we don't deserve it. Going forwards, we don't expect harmony either. A house divided against itself cannot stand. So, it is our intention to release you from the captivity we have imposed upon you."

One of the nefeshchayans yelled out, "Hey, you realise you're currently *our* prisoner, don't you?"

Polkingbeal67 acknowledged the interruption with a nod. "You will be permitted to return to Earth at the earliest opportunity and you go with our blessing. May the presence of Mortian Karma 5 in the DNA of your children protect future generations of your people from the evil designs of the chilloks."

To say I was dumbfounded is an understatement to rival the most jaw-dropping ones you can think of.

John got up, solemnly shook the Mortian leader's hand and clasped his shoulder. "For our part, we thank you for this gesture. It bodes well for the future relations between our two peoples. We 'ave debated our options at great length and I beg leave to inform you that, with your permission, we would like to remain 'ere on this planet."

A few spots of rain started falling, which then turned into light drizzle. Ollie leaned across to me and whispered, "We don't like the way the pie gets shared out on Earth. We deserve a better world. We're gonna stick with camelism."

Well, that settled it – I was clearly the most awesome mediator in the entire history of intergalactic mediations. And it had just come so naturally to me! The light drizzle turned into heavy drizzle, and, before very long, the rain poured down, as if Theta Flying Pigs was squeezing the clouds like wet sponges. For several minutes, I basked in the exhilarating downpour - immersed in a daze of self-aggrandisement - until yukawa3 started cavorting around the yard, singing 'We Are Family', the Sister Sledge song with which he'd become familiar during his short stay with me on Earth. And it wasn't long before several others were joining him, nefeshchayans and Mortians alike, singing and dancing in the rain. Oh, and cartwheels. Yukawa3 started doing cartwheels.

. . .

Polkingbeal67's new-found capacity for altruism and empathy toward earthlings was not yet exhausted. Taking me to one side he informed me, with words so softly spoken I had to bend down to hear them, that one of the Mortians was prepared to submit to a surgical exchange of hearts, enabling me to return to Earth. It would exactly correspond to the procedure that was undertaken to allow my grandmother to return home all those years ago. For some reason, I assumed the volunteer, who had apparently expressed a wish to remain anonymous, was smolin10. Given his predecessor's connection with my family, this totally made sense to me.

You'd think that I would have jumped at the chance, without a second's hesitation. But thoughts of Aysha nibbled away at me.

It was as if polkingbeal67 could read my mind. "You're having a change of heart," he said with a knowing nod of his head. Surely, he didn't intend the double meaning? "You're reluctant to leave your friend," he continued sympathetically. "Don't stand by the water and long for fish. Go home and weave a net."

At first, I thought this was a well-meaning entreaty to accept my loss and rebuild my life on Earth. But as I watched his corpulent frame disappear indoors, something hit me with the clarity of an epiphany.

Later the same day, after I'd said my goodbyes, casimir2 and I took a hovercruiser to the wormhole gateway complex. Several other cruisers followed us across the plains. The last rays of the larger of the two suns lingered in the western sky and the orange glow created a double rainbow in the receding clouds to the east. I leaped out of my seat, blood pounding in my veins, and ran through the corridors as if I was deranged. Retrieving the gold necklace, I retraced my steps even faster until I passed casimir2, who was preparing for the surgery in a pair of anterooms close to the entrance. I paused for a second, then flew outside to catch the sunset before it vanished below the horizon. Holding the necklace aloft, I searched the skies in vain for several minutes. Nothing. Deeply dismayed, I trudged back towards the entrance, glancing back every few paces. I almost trod on her before I noticed her, preening her wings in the corner of the doorway.

. . .

The next thing I recall is coming round after the operation. Casimir2 was leaning over me, and an autosurgery android whirled away like a mechanised mantis. I was in no pain whatsoever, and I was in good spirits. Ignoring his oozing, rubbery, pustular skin, I sat up and embraced casimir2 with all the fervour of my soul.

"We can proceed with the transit configuration as soon as you feel up to it," he told me. "And I've worked out the parameters for the particle reassembly of your friend."

Aysha flew down and perched on my shoulder. As we walked towards the room that housed the wormhole control desk, I peered into the second anteroom hoping for a reassuring glimpse of smolin10 in recovery mode.

I couldn't see the treatment table, but what I *could* see stunned the breath out of me. I will never forget the sight for as long as I live – a small magma table containing a snapped yellow and navy golf umbrella, a crystal necklace, an eye patch and a sherg-encrusted helmet.

. . .

"Oh, here we go again! Weird, weird, weird. This definitely feels like Schrödinger's box. Y'know, conceptually? Actually, I guess it was like that when you were a pigeon? Nobody knew if you were dead or alive. It was so spooky. Don't you think that whole thing was exactly like you were Schrödinger's cat?"

"I was alive. And, Neil, don't say it. Please don't suggest I might 'ave been a cat among the pigeons. I wasn't a cat. I was a pigeon."

"Okay, well, Schrödinger's pigeon then?"

"Really? Schrödinger's pigeon? Didn't Schrödinger's box 'ave a 'ammer in it? Tell you what, if I 'ad a 'ammer right now, I'd clock you over the 'ead with it! Could you pass me my necklace, please?"

Other books by David Winship

Through The Wormhole, Literally, 2015, ISBN 978-1508718406

ANTidote, 2016, ISBN 978-1530860722

Stirring The Grass, 2016, ISBN 978-1492952725

Off The Frame, 2001, ISBN 978-1482793833

Talking Trousers and Other Stories, 2013, ISBN 978-1484898420